The It girl

Created by Cecily von Ziegesar

The It girl

created by
Cecily von Ziegesar

headline

First published in 2005 by
Little, Brown and Company, USA

First published in paperback in Great Britain in 2007 by
HEADLINE PUBLISHING GROUP

11

ALLOYENTERTAINMENT

Produced by Alloy Entertainment,
151 West 26th Street, New York, NY 10001

Cataloguing in Publication Data is available from the British Library

ISBN 978 0 7553 3997 6

Typeset in Garamond 3 by Palimpsest Book Production Limited, Grangemouth,
Stirlingshire

Printed and bound in Great Britain by Clays Ltd, Elcograf S.p.A.

Headline's policy is to use papers that are
natural, renewable and recyclable products and made from
wood grown in sustainable forests. The logging and manufacturing processes are
expected to conform to the environmental regulations
of the country of origin.

HEADLINE PUBLISHING GROUP
An Hachette Livre UK Company
338 Euston Road
London NW1 3BH

www.headline.co.uk
www.hachettelivre.co.uk

I've never let my school interfere with my education.

Mark Twain

A WAVERLY OWL DOES NOT DISCUSS
HALF-NAKEDNESS WITH STRANGERS.

Somebody's plaid Jack Spade duffel slammed into Jenny Humphrey's shin and jerked her out of a dream. The 10 A.M. Amtrak Empire Service to Rhinecliff, New York, had stopped in Poughkeepsie, and a tall, twentyish, stubbly chinned boy in dark brown square Paul Smith glasses and a Decemberists T-shirt was standing over her.

'Anybody sitting here?' he asked.

'Nope,' she responded groggily, scooting over. He threw his bag under the seat and settled in next to Jenny.

The train groaned along at about a mile an hour. Jenny sniffed at the stale, slightly sweaty train car air and jiggled her foot, thinking about how she was going to be super-late for check-in at Waverly Academy. She would've been early if her dad, Rufus, had driven her up here in his blue beater Volvo wagon — he'd practically begged Jenny to let him — but Jenny hadn't wanted her unshaven, peacenik father to drop her off at her brand-new, haute boarding school. Knowing him, he'd have tried to start up an impromptu poetry slam with her new classmates and shown off old pictures of Jenny when she was a lame seventh grader and wore nothing but fluorescent green and orange Old Navy fleeces. Um, no thanks.

'Going to Waverly?' the boy asked. He raised his eyebrows at the *Waverly Academy Guide to Ethics* that sat unopened in Jenny's lap.

Jenny brushed a brown tendril out of her eyes. 'Yeah,' she answered. 'I'm starting there this year.' She couldn't hide the enthusiasm in her voice — she was so excited to start her brand-new boarding school that she felt all jiggly inside, like she had to pee.

'Freshman?'

'Nope. Sophomore. I used to go to Constance Billard. It's in the city.' Jenny was a little pleased that she had a relatively chic past to refer to, or that it at least sounded that way.

'So you wanted a change of pace, or what?' He fiddled with the strap of his worn leather watchband.

Jenny shrugged. This boy looked like he was her brother Dan's age. Dan had just taken off for Evergreen College on the West Coast two days ago, taking nothing with him except for two duffel bags, his Mac G4 laptop, and two cartons of cigarettes. Jenny, on the other hand, had already shipped four oversize boxes and a couple of giant duffels to Waverly, and had lugged a giant suitcase and an overstuffed bag with her. In her hyperexcited preparation for boarding school, she had practically bought out the hair, cosmetics, and feminine products aisles at CVS – who knew what she'd need at boarding school! She'd also gone on a buying spree at Club Monaco, J.Crew, and Barneys with the credit card her dad had lent her for back-to-school shopping. 'Kinda,' she finally answered.

The truth was, she'd been asked to leave Constance – apparently because she was considered a 'bad influence' on the other girls. Jenny hadn't thought she was being a bad influence at all – she was just trying to have fun, like every other girl at school. But somehow, all of her moments of extreme fun had also been highly publicized and embarrassing: a picture of her boobs in a sports bra had shown up in a magazine (she'd thought it was a sportswear model shoot), a Webcast of her practically naked butt had been spread around the school, and she'd made some bad decisions about which boys she should make out with at various parties – and of course everybody had found out.

The final straw had come after Jenny had spent a night at the Plaza Hotel with her brother's old band, the Raves. A photograph of her leaving the Plaza in nothing but a fluffy white bathrobe had appeared online on Page Six the next day. Rumors had flown that Jenny was sleeping with *all* the Raves, *including* her brother. Ew! Concerned parents quickly called up the Constance headmistress, aflutter about

Jenny's promiscuity. After all, Constance had a reputation for excellence to uphold!

Although Jenny hadn't even been with *one* Rave, let alone all of them, she hadn't exactly wanted to *deny* the rumor – she kind of loved that everyone was talking about her. So as she'd sat with the Constance Billard headmistress, Ms McLean, in her patriotic red, white and blue office back in the city, Jenny had realized something huge: it wasn't the end of the world to get kicked out of Constance. This was her chance to start over, to reinvent herself as the blunder-free sophisticate she'd always wanted to be. And where was the classiest place to start over? Boarding school, of course.

Much to her dad's chagrin – she was pretty sure Rufus wanted her to live with him in their Upper West Side apartment forever – Jenny had rabidly researched a whole bunch of schools and toured a few. The first school had turned out to have a strict disciplinary code and had been too boring for words. Within minutes of getting to the second school, on the other hand, she'd been offered Ecstasy and had taken her top off. But just like the third bed for Goldilocks, the third school that Jenny had tested, Waverly, was just right.

Well, to tell the truth, she hadn't actually visited Waverly – she'd run out of time, applied way past the deadline, and taken some creative liberties with her application – but she'd looked at thousands of pictures online and memorized all the building names and campus maps. She was certain it would be perfect.

'I used to go to Waverly's rival,' the boy said, pulling a book out of his bag. 'St Lucius. Our school hated your school.'

'Oh,' Jenny replied quietly, sinking into her seat.

'I'm kidding.' He smiled and turned back to his book. Jenny noticed it was Henry Miller's *Tropic of Cancer*, one of her dad's favorites. According to Rufus, it had been banned because it was too right-on in its vicious social commentary about love and sex in New York City. Hello, sex scenes. Jenny felt her cheeks growing pink.

Then she realized: she was acting like her old, unsophisticated self. And one thing was for sure: Old Jenny obviously wasn't working for her.

Jenny studied the boy carefully. She didn't know him and would probably never see him again, so why did she care what he thought of her? At Waverly, Jenny was going to be stunning, amazing New Jenny, the girl who belonged at the center of everything.

So why not become New Jenny starting *right now*?

Mustering up her courage, she uncrossed her arms to reveal her rather large double-D chest, which seemed even bigger, since she was barely five feet tall, and sat up straight. 'So, um, any good parts in that book?'

The boy looked puzzled, his eyes darting back and forth from Jenny's innocent face to her chest to the worn paperback's cover. Finally, he wrinkled his nose and answered, 'Maybe.'

'Will you read some to me?'

The boy licked his lips. 'Okay. But only if you read me

a line from that book you've got there first.' He tapped the maroon cover of her beloved *Waverly Academy Guide to Ethics*.

'Sure.' Jenny opened the rule book. She'd received it a few weeks ago and had devoured it cover to cover. She loved its plush leather binding, its creamy paper stock, and the nursery-rhymey, slightly condescending, slightly British style in which it was written. It sounded so wonderfully proper and upscale, and Jenny was sure that by the time she'd even spent a few weeks at Waverly, she'd be as polished, graceful, and perfect as Amanda Hearst, the young socialite, or the late Carolyn Bessette Kennedy.

She cleared her throat. 'Here's a good one. "Waverly Owls may not dance in a sexually suggestive manner in public."' She laughed. Did that mean they could dance in a sexually suggestive manner in *private*?

'Do they really refer to you as Waverly Owls?' The boy leaned over to look at the page. He smelled like Ivory soap.

'Yes!' As she said it, Jenny grinned. She, Jenny Humphrey, was going to be a Waverly Owl!

She turned the page. '"Waverly Owls are not permitted sexual intimacy. A Waverly Owl must not engage in activities that might be dangerous, such as jumping off the Richards Bridge. A Waverly Owl does not wear spaghetti straps or miniskirts above midthigh."'

The boy snickered. 'When they're talking about a girl, shouldn't it be an Owlette?'

Jenny slammed the book shut. 'Okay. Now it's your turn.'

'Well, I just started, so I'll read from the beginning.'

The boy smirked and opened to the first page. '"From the very beginning, I have trained myself not to want anything too badly."'

Funny, Jenny thought. She had the opposite problem – she wanted everything *way* too badly.

'"I was corrupt,"' he continued. '"Corrupt from the start."'

'I'm corrupt!' Jenny blurted out. 'But not from the start.' Old Jenny couldn't believe what New Jenny was saying.

'Yeah?' He closed the book. 'I'm Sam, by the way.'

'Jenny.' She looked down to see if Sam wanted her to shake his hand, but it was still wedged under his leg. They both smiled awkwardly.

'So, does your corruptness have anything to do with why you're leaving New York for boarding school?' Sam asked.

'Maybe.' Jenny shrugged, trying to be coy and mysterious at the same time.

'Spill.'

She let out a sigh. She could admit the truth, but *Everybody thought I was sleeping with all the guys in this band, and I didn't deny it* sounded kind of slutty. Definitely not mysterious or chic. So instead she decided to take some creative liberties. 'Well, I was in a sort of risqué fashion show.'

Sam's eyes glittered with interest. 'What do you mean?'

She thought for a moment. 'Well, for one look, I just had this bra-and-underwear set on. And heels. I guess it was a little too much for some people.'

This wasn't entirely a lie. Jenny *had* modeled last year – for a Les Best spread in *W* magazine. Clothed. But clothes didn't seem too interesting at the moment.

'Really?' Sam cleared his throat and readjusted his glasses. 'Have you heard of Tinsley Carmichael? You should know her.'

'Who?'

'Tinsley Carmichael. She goes to Waverly. I go to Bard now, but I met her a couple times at parties last year . . . She came to school in her own seaplane. But someone told me she decided to leave Waverly because Wes Anderson offered her the lead in his next movie.'

Jenny shrugged, feeling strangely competitive with – and a wee bit excited about – this Tinsley girl. She sounded like the ideal New Jenny.

The exhausted-looking train conductor stomped down the aisle and grabbed the ticket off the top of her seat. 'Rhinecliff, next.'

'Oh. This is me.' Jenny took a deep breath. It was really happening! She looked out the window, expecting to see something truly magical, but saw only lush green trees, a wide field, and telephone poles. Still, trees! A field! The only field in Manhattan was Sheep Meadow in Central Park, and it was always filled with drug dealers and really skinny half-naked girls sunbathing.

She stood and reached for her red and white polka-dotted soft-shell LeSportsac bag and the old-school brown Samsonite suitcase she'd borrowed from her dad. It had a big HUGS NOT BOMBS sticker next to the handles. Not very New Jenny.

As she struggled to bring the case to the ground, Sam stood to help her, pulling it effortlessly off the rack.

'Thanks,' she said, blushing.

'No problem.' He pushed the hair out of his eyes. 'So, do I get to see pictures of you at . . . at the fashion show?'

'If you search online,' Jenny lied. She stared out the window and saw, across a field, an old rooster weathervane on the top of a large, faded farmhouse. 'The designer's name is, um, Rooster.'

'Never heard of him.'

'He's kind of obscure,' Jenny answered quickly, noting that the polished, pink Polo-wearing boy sitting behind them was definitely listening to their conversation. Jenny tried to see what he was typing on his BlackBerry, but he covered the screen when he noticed her watching him.

'You . . . you should come to Bard sometime,' Sam continued. 'We have some killer parties. Great DJs and stuff.'

'Okay,' Jenny replied over her shoulder, raising her eyebrows just a touch. 'Although, you know, a Waverly Owl isn't allowed to dance in a sexually suggestive manner.'

'I won't tell on you,' he answered, not taking his eyes off her chest.

''Bye, Sam,' Jenny waved, using her most flirty, musical voice. She stepped off the train onto the platform and sucked in a deep breath of fresh country air. *Whoa*.

New Jenny would take a little getting used to!

OwlNet   Instant Message Inbox

RyanReynolds: Hey, Benster. Welcome back, girl!

BennyCunningham: Hey, sweetie! How's life?

RyanReynolds: I had the worst ride up here in our plane. My dad has this maniac pilot and they were yakking at each other the whole time and going faster and faster . . .

BennyCunningham: Next time you should fly with me. I'll let you snuggle with me under my pashmina.

RyanReynolds: God, you're a tease. Hey, did u c Callie's pic in Atlanta Magazine?

BennyCunningham: No, but I heard it nearly ruined her mom. She had to do damage control on Good Morning Atlanta!

RyanReynolds: Yeah, C looks bombed in the pic.

BennyCunningham: Is she still with EZ? I'm going to jump him if she's not.

RyanReynolds: Dunno. Someone told me they saw him dancing with some gorgeous girl with really blue eyes and black dreads in Lexington.

BennyCunningham: Sorta sounds like Tinsley. Except for the dreads.

RyanReynolds: I know. Too bad she won't be at the party tonight.

BennyCunningham: Seriously.

2

A WAVERLY OWL SHOULD RESIST THE
URGE TO LICK HER BOYFRIEND FROM
HEAD TO TOE.

Callie Vernon set her luggage down in the entranceway to Dumbarton dorm room 303 and looked around. The room was exactly as she, Brett and Tinsley had left it — except for the lack of empty Diet Coke bottles, Parliament butt-filled ashtrays, and CD cases strewn all over the room. Last fall, because they'd only been sophomores, Callie and her two best friends, Brett Messerschmidt and Tinsley Carmichael, had been assigned a horrible, cramped room with only one window. But then Tinsley had bribed three dorky senior girls to switch with them the first week of school by promising them invites to the best secret parties. They'd wanted this room because it was bigger than most, with casement windows overlooking the Hudson River, and because it was close to the fire escape – ideal for sneaking out after curfew.

Brett hadn't arrived back at school yet, and Tinsley had been expelled at the end of school last year. They'd been caught on Ecstasy in the middle of the rugby fields at five in the morning by Mr Purcell, the uptight physics teacher, who liked going running with his three impeccably groomed giant schnauzers before sunrise. It was the first time they'd ever tried E, and it had taken them a moment to stop laughing at the ridiculous-looking dogs before realizing what enormous trouble they were in. The girls had all been called into the headmaster's office separately – first Tinsley, then Callie, then Brett – but the only one to get in any real trouble was Tinsley, who was promptly booted out of Waverly.

Callie caught a glimpse of herself in the just-Windexed mirror over the antique oak bureau and straightened her white Jill Stuart shell top and pleated lemon-yellow Tocca skirt. She'd lost a few pounds over the summer and the side zipper kept sliding around to her belly button. Callie was thin now, maybe a little too thin, and freckly from the summer. Her hair was long and shaggy, and her round, hazel eyes were fanned by thick, blond-tipped eyelashes. She puckered her lips, blew a kiss at the mirror, and felt an anxious flutter in her chest.

All this summer, Callie's mind had spun, thinking about why Tinsley had been expelled and she and Brett hadn't been. Had Brett set it up that way? Brett was super-secretive about her life at home – her mom and dad never came to Parents' Day, and Brett never invited anybody to her house in East Hampton for long weekends. Tinsley had once dropped a hint that Brett had some family issues she didn't want anybody to know about. Could Brett really have orchestrated Tinsley's expulsion so she wouldn't expose her secrets? It sounded totally soap-operaish, but Brett was so melodramatic sometimes that Callie wouldn't put it past her.

Callie nestled into her desk chair, actually glad to be back at school. Beyond not talking to her two best friends – she hadn't heard a peep from either of them – her summer had been a disaster. First, there'd been the *Atlanta Magazine* photo of Callie at Club Compound, dancing on a table with a vanilla Martini in her hand. The caption read, *Overserved and underage: Is this appropriate behavior for a governor's daughter?* Needless to say, that hadn't gone over well with her mother's conservative Georgian voters. Oops.

After that nightmare, Callie had flown to her family's chalet in Barcelona – Mr Vernon was part Spanish and spent his summers working on real estate deals in Europe. She had hoped that Barcelona would be the perfect backdrop for a romantic rendezvous with her boyfriend, Easy Walsh. But that visit had been anything but romantic. Try freaky.

'Hey,' came a gravelly voice behind her.

Callie wheeled around. Easy. There he was, all rumpled, sexy six feet of him, standing in her doorway, looking more gorgeous than ever.

'Oh!' She felt her palms get slick with sweat.

'How are you?' he asked, pulling at the worn hem of

his polo shirt. His glossy almost-black hair curled around his neck and ears.

'Confused' would have been a reasonable answer. The last time she'd seen Easy was when she'd dropped him off at the Barcelona airport. They hadn't kissed goodbye, and they'd barely even spoken the whole last day of his visit.

'Fine,' she replied cautiously. 'How did you get in here? Did Angelica see you?' Her dorm mistress, Angelica Pardee, was really strict about allowing boys in the all-girls' dorm except during 'visitation,' which was only for an hour between sports practice and dinner.

'You look too skinny,' Easy said softly, ignoring Callie's questions.

Callie frowned. 'Do you want to get into trouble on the first day of school?'

'Your boobs are going away,' he continued.

'God,' she muttered in annoyance. The truth was, she hadn't been hungry all summer – not even for Barcelona-style paella, her favorite. She was too nervous to eat, or to do much of anything, really. The last few weeks in Spain she'd spent on the couch, looking like an unstructured slob, wearing her slightly ragged, white Dior string bikini and some old ripped batik sarong she'd picked up for next to nothing in a Barcelona outdoor market, watching hours and hours of *The Surreal Life* in Spanish. And she didn't even speak much Spanish. 'What are you doing back so soon?'

Easy was usually fashionably late to Waverly check-in – another no-no – because he arrived in a tractor-trailer with his Thoroughbred, Credo, whom he kept on campus.

'Credo's coming next week, so there was no reason for me to be late.'

He looked at Callie. They'd been together since last fall, but he'd had a hard time getting psyched to see her back at school after his parents had received an angry note from Dean Marymount over the summer saying he'd be watching Easy carefully this year. Apparently there were rules to uphold, and just because Easy was a legacy – his grandfather, father, and three older brothers had all attended Waverly – didn't mean he could bend those rules. So instead of heading up to school a week late with Credo, Easy had flown alone on a chartered plane from Kentucky to New York with leather reclining seats and unlimited champagne. Sounds great, right? Except it wasn't exactly what Easy had had in mind.

Easy regularly fantasized about getting kicked out of Waverly Academy – until he remembered his father's bargain. If Easy graduated from Waverly, he could take a postgraduate year in Paris. His father even had a big apartment in the Latin Quarter all ready for Easy's year abroad. Paris – how cool would that be? He'd drink absinthe, paint street scenes from his bedroom window, and ride along the Seine on an ancient, rickety Peugeot bike, a Gauloise hanging from his mouth. He could smoke his brains out and nobody would give him shit for it!

'You going to the party at Richards' lounge tonight?' Callie asked.

Easy shrugged. 'Not sure.' He stood just inside the door frame.

Callie pulled a foot out of her pointy-toed Burberry loafer and rolled her ballerina-pink painted toes against the floor. A horrible feeling of dread washed over her. *Why* wouldn't Easy want to go to the first party of the year? *Everybody* went to the first party of the year. Was he seeing someone else? Someone he wanted to be alone with on the first night of school?

'Well, I'm going,' she said quickly, crossing her arms.

Neither one had made a move toward the other. But with his mussed hair, broad shoulders, and golden-brown forearms, Easy looked so irresistible, Callie was dying to lick him from head to toe.

'Did you have a good summer after Spain?' she squeaked, trying to sound as indifferent as possible.

'I guess. Lexington was ass-boring as usual.' He pulled a toothpick from behind his ear and placed it between his slightly chapped lips.

Callie leaned against her antique white-painted wood bed frame. His visit to Spain had been tainted from the start. Easy had had to fly coach class, and when he'd arrived, he'd been terse and gruff and had headed straight to the bar – not one of those cute little outdoor cafés straight out of *The Sun Also Rises*, but simply the closest bar possible, at the airport. Then he'd passed out on the Vernons' couch, which was a real problem since Callie's dad *needed* to sit on that couch to watch the international feed of CNN every single minute he wasn't working.

Callie tilted her hips forward and chewed on her freshly manicured thumbnail. 'Well, that's nice,' she responded finally. She wished she could just wrap her arms around him and kiss him everywhere, but she couldn't exactly do that when he hadn't even tried to hug her hello.

Then she spied a familiar figure behind Easy and her heart started racing.

'Mr Walsh!' crowed Angelica Pardee, Dumbarton's dorm mistress. Angelica wasn't even thirty, but she seemed to be in a hurry to enter middle age. Today she was wearing a thin, shapeless tan cardigan, a straight, knee-length black skirt, and sensible black Easy Spirits. Her calves were a little veiny and way too bluish-white, and she wore no makeup. 'Do I have to report you already?'

Easy jumped. 'I'm sorry,' he apologized, dazedly pressing his hand to his head, as if he had amnesia. 'I haven't been here in so long, and, like, I forgot which dorm I was in.' He looked across the room, directly into Callie's eyes, and she felt her arms goose-bump.

'See you later?' she finally mouthed.

He nodded ever so slightly.

'Stables?' she whispered.

'Tomorrow?' he mouthed back.

'Why not tonight?' Callie wanted to ask. But she didn't.

'Mr *Walsh*!' Angelica practically spat, gripping the cuff of his shirt. Her face was an abnormal red.

'Okay!' Easy yelped. 'I *said* I was leaving.'

Angelica shook her head and ushered Easy down the hall.

Callie turned and stared out the window. The abandoned stables were where they used to go last year to fool around.

Only a few students kept horses at school, so several of the stalls were always empty. She hated that she had had to suggest they meet there, and not the other way around.

Droves of freshmen lumbered up Dumbarton's steps, carrying way too much luggage. Callie noticed how overwhelmed the girls seemed. She could relate. There were so many things about boarding school that you couldn't plan for. They'd soon discover that they didn't need half their shit and that they had forgotten the really important stuff – like empty shampoo bottles to hide vodka in. She watched the throng of freshman girls part as Easy strolled down the Dumbarton steps, nodding to the new, innocent faces. God, it was hard dating such a flirt.

She put her head in her hands. It was so obvious what had gone wrong in Spain. The last night they'd spent together, she'd admitted something to Easy that was so big and so *scary* for her to say. And what had been his answer? Nothing. Silence.

Callie sighed. They'd have to talk about it tomorrow, although she hoped they'd be doing a lot more than just talking.

OwlNet   Instant Message Inbox

BennyCunningham: My brother's friend at Exeter told me there's a new girl at Waverly who's a stripper from NYC.

HeathFerro: ?!?

BennyCunningham: Yep. Some club named . . . Hen Party? Chicken Hut? Horse Stable? I think in Brooklyn? I had my cousin who lives in the Village look it up – it's the kind of place where u take it all off. Thong included.

HeathFerro: When can I meet her?

BennyCunningham: Heath, you're nasty.

HeathFerro: Don't you know it, baby!

3

A WAVERLY OWL SHOULD KEEP HER
GRANNY BRAS HIDDEN AT ALL TIMES.

'Right here is fine,' Jenny told the cabdriver as soon as she spied the discreet maroon sign reading WAVERLY ACADEMY hanging from a tree next to a tiny, one-story brick building. Waverly wasn't far from the train station, but Jenny hadn't been able to get here fast enough.

'You sure?' The cabdriver turned around, revealing a thin beaky nose and a faded light blue Yankees cap. 'Because the front office is—'

'I'm a student here,' Jenny interrupted, feeling a thrill ripple through her chest as she spoke. 'I know where the front office is.'

The cabdriver threw up his hands in defeat. 'You're the

boss.' Jenny handed him a twenty, stepped out of the cab, and looked around.

She was *here*. Waverly. The grass seemed greener, the trees taller, and the sky cleaner and bluer than anywhere she'd ever been before. There were lush evergreens on all sides, and on her right was a wide, cobblestone path snaking up a hill. A green field spread out to her left, and in the distance a few boys in Abercrombie fatigue shorts were kicking around a soccer ball. The whole place *smelled* of boarding school. Like the deep woods, which she'd only been in a few times, before she knew better than to accompany her dad and his kooky anarchist buddies on camping trips in southern Vermont.

A cream-colored Mercedes convertible swept past her. She heard a stately clock tower bong out one o'clock.

'Yes,' she whispered, hugging herself. She had definitely arrived.

The truth was, she'd wanted to get out of the cab because she couldn't wait a second longer to plant her feet on Waverly ground, not because she knew exactly where she was going. Staring at the little brick building beside her, she realized that ivy had grown over the windows and the door was rusted shut. This definitely wasn't the front office, where she needed to check in. Another car, this one a battleship-gray Bentley, passed her. Jenny decided to follow the parade of luxury cars.

She dragged her bags up the freshly mowed hill, her kitten heels sinking into the slightly wet, springy lawn. A running track circled off to her right, flanked by tall white bleachers. A few girls were running briskly around the track, their ponytails bouncing. At the top of the hill, above the dark green trees, she could see a white church spire and the slate roofs of some more redbrick buildings. The boys with the soccer ball had stopped playing and were now standing together, staring in her direction. Were they staring at *her*?

'D'you need a ride?' a male voice interrupted her thoughts. Jenny looked over, and saw a tan, middle-aged man with dazzling white teeth hanging out the driver-side window of a silver Cadillac Escalade. She could see her reflection in his Ray-Ban aviator sunglasses. She looked awkward and silly wearing a too-tight Lacoste cotton polo shirt and dragging her luggage up the hill in a pair of pointy pink kitten-heel sandals. She'd bought the shirt at Bloomingdale's because she'd been sure it would make her feel like she absolutely belonged at boarding school, and she had gone back to visit the sandals several times before they finally went on sale so she could buy them.

'Um, sure. I'm going to the front office.' She slid into the backseat of the SUV, which smelled like new car. A dirty-blond boy with chiseled features was sitting in the passenger seat looking sulky, but he didn't twist around to speak to her.

'I don't know, Heath,' the man told the boy quietly. 'You may not be able to have the party – your mother and I might need the Woodstock house that weekend.'

'Mother*fucker*,' the boy hissed under is breath. His father sighed.

Jenny barely acknowledged the boy's rudeness. She only had ears for one word: party.

She felt funny, though, asking the boy about it, since he seemed pretty pissed off. The car stopped at an enormous redbrick building with a small maroon sign next to the stone pathway that said FRONT OFFICE. Jenny squeaked her thanks, grabbed her bags, and made a beeline for the door.

Inside, the waiting room was ballroom size, with shiny floors made of dark cherry wood. A large crystal chandelier hung from the double-height ceiling. Four butter-colored leather couches were arranged in a square around a heavy teak coffee table, and a beautiful, amber-haired boy was stretched out on one of them, reading *FHM* and eating a bag of Fritos.

'Can I help you?' someone asked behind her. Jenny jumped. She turned and saw a Laura Ashley-clad older woman with a very hairsprayed gray bob and watery blue eyes wearing a name tag that read HELLO, MY NAME IS MRS TULLINGTON sitting behind a desk with a little white sign that read NEW STUDENTS' CHECK-IN.

'Hi!' Jenny peeped. 'I'm Jennifer Humphrey. I'm a new student!'

She studied the *Welcome to Waverly* schedule that was taped to the desk. School didn't officially begin until tomorrow night at the orientation welcome dinner, but sports team tryouts would take place tomorrow during the day. Mrs Tullington typed some information into a pristine, gunmetal-gray Sony laptop, and then she frowned. 'There's a problem.'

Jenny stared at her blankly. *Problem*? There were no problems in magical Waverly land! Look at how gorgeous that Frito-eating boy was!

'We have you down as a boy,' Mrs Tullington continued.

'Wait, what?' Jenny snapped back to consciousness. 'Did you say a *boy*?'

'Yes . . . we have you here as *Mr* Jennifer Humphrey.' The older woman seemed flustered, flipping papers back and forth. 'Some students have very old family names, you see, and maybe the admissions committee thought Jennifer was—'

'Oh,' Jenny replied self-consciously, twisting around to see if the boy on the couch had heard, but he was gone. All the Waverly mail she'd gotten had been addressed to a Mr Jennifer Humphrey. She'd assumed it was just a typo. What a dumb thing to assume. *So* Old Jenny. 'What does that mean? I had all my bags shipped to the . . . the Richards dorm, I think it was?'

'Yes, but that's the boys' dorm.' Mrs Tullington explained this slowly, as if Jenny didn't get it. 'We'll have to find another space for you.' She flipped through some papers. 'The girls' dorms are all filled up . . .' She picked up the phone. 'We'll sort this out. But go see if your things are in the Richards dorm. They would have been sent to the lounge on the first floor – that's where all mailed luggage is held. It's down the path to your right, fourth building. There's a sign. We'll send someone for you once we figure this out.'

'Okay,' Jenny replied happily, picturing all the hot, shirt-less preppy boys she was about to see lounging around Richards. 'No problem.'

'The main door should be open. But don't go into any of the rooms. They're off limits!' Mrs Tullington called after her.

'Of course,' Jenny agreed. 'Thank you!'

Jenny stood on the stone porch of the front office. From studying the campus maps, she'd learned that Waverly's dorms, chapel, auditorium and classrooms were all laid out in a big circle, with the soccer fields in the center. At the back of the circle were the crew houses, the Hudson River, the art gallery, the botany labs, and the library. All of the buildings seemed to be made of brick, with old, heavy windows and white trim.

Strolling excitedly toward the dorms, Jenny had to will herself not to skip. Girls in beat-up Citizens jeans and ragged grosgrain flip-flops were spilling out of Mercedes SUVs and Audi wagons, hugging other girls and talking excitedly about what had happened over the summer at their country houses on Martha's Vineyard and in the Hamptons. Boys in zip-up hooded sweatshirts and camo shorts were ramming into each other with their shoulders. One guy carrying a Louis Vuitton duffel shouted, 'I did so much E this summer, my brain is fried!'

Jenny felt her body stiffen, suddenly intimidated. Everyone looked so beautiful – scrubbed and clean and fashionable without even *trying* to be, which was so much cooler than spending hours primping, like she usually did – and like they'd known one another forever. Jenny took a deep breath and continued along the path.

Then, out of nowhere, a giant potatolike thing swooped down, making a horrific cawing noise, and flew about an inch from Jenny's face.

'Aghh!' she screamed, swatting in front of her.

She watched as the thing soared into a tree. Scary! It looked like a rat on steroids.

Behind her, Jenny heard a snicker and wheeled around. All the girls were still talking to one another, but two boys in backwards W baseball caps were sitting on a stone wall, watching. Then she noticed that in her fright, she'd dropped her overpacked suitcase on the path, and it had sprung open. *Oh, God.* Her giant nude extra-support bras, the kind with the extra hook-and-eye clasp and padded straps that she had to use when she had her period, were all over the ground. They were bras a huge, dumpy grandmother might wear.

She quickly shoved the bras back in her suitcase, peeking to see if the two boys sitting on the wall had noticed. They were already greeting some other guy in a white baseball cap, doing that hand-grab half-hug thing that guys do, not paying any attention to Jenny. With the fresh air and lush, rambling scenery, maybe oversized boobs and bras weren't the kind of thing Waverly kids noticed . . .

Then the new arrival turned to Jenny and touched the brim of his ratty white baseball cap with his index finger. He gave her a wink, as if to say, *The air might be fresh, but we're not totally blind.*

4

WAVERLY OWLS KNOW THAT CLEAN LUNGS MAKE FOR HEALTHY HOOTING!

Brandon Buchanan sat on one of his Samsonites and stared at Heath Ferro. No matter when he arrived on campus, he always saw Heath first. Even though they were roommates, Brandon found Heath really annoying most of the time.

'I brought a carton of smokes,' Heath bragged as he unzipped his black medium-size Tumi duffel and showed Brandon the edge of the Camel 'unfiltered' box. They were in Richards' lounge, waiting to get room assignments. It was just a normal common room – the meeting spot where the guys watched *SportsCenter*, shared sausage pizzas from Ritoli's, and flirted with cute girls during visiting hour – but still, the lounge felt English and regal.

The cream-colored plaster ceilings were fifteen feet high, with dark wooden beams, and there were comfortable, worn leather armchairs scattered all over the place. An old cabinet TV that got three network stations and, randomly, ESPN, loomed in the corner. On the floor lay a huge, ornate Oriental carpet. Careless cigarette burn holes made the rug look even more historic.

'That'll last you about a week,' Brandon scoffed, pushing his short wavy golden-brown hair back into its deliberately tousled place. Heath smoked like a fiend right outside Richards even though smoking was forbidden on campus, but the faculty constantly looked the other way. It might've been because of Heath's stunning good looks – he was tall, lean, and athletic, with gold-flecked green eyes, sharp cheek-bones, and shaggy dark blond hair. But more likely, it was Heath's family that kept him out of trouble. Heath's father had donated four and a half million dollars for the Olympic-size natatorium and another million for a three-floor addition to the renovated botany library, so Heath could pretty much do as he damn well pleased and never get so much as a warning.

'You bring your weird girly cream with you this year?' Heath teased.

'It's moisturizer,' Brandon clarified.

'It's moisturizer,' Heath echoed in a high-pitched voice.

So what if Brandon took good care of his skin? And liked nice clothes and shoes and liked his wavy hair to be just so? He was neurotic about his height – he was only five-eight – and shaved his chest because he hated the tiny little hairs that grew in the caved-in part of his breastbone. His less-clean friends busted on him to no end. But so what?

'Who do you think they're gonna room us with?' Heath asked.

'Don't know. Maybe Ryan. Unless he gets a single again.' Ryan Reynolds's father had invented the soft contact lens and openly used his wealth as leverage to his son's advantage. Lots of kids' parents bribed the school, but usually it was kept a secret.

Heath snickered. 'Maybe you'll get paired up with Walsh.'

'Nah, even the administration knows better than that,' Brandon replied. Just the sound of that name – Walsh, as in Easy Walsh – made Brandon's blood curdle.

'So, how's Natasha?' Heath recited her name with a bad Russian accent.

Brandon sighed. Last April he had started going out with Natasha Wood, who went to Millbrook Academy, after Easy stole his old girlfriend, Callie Vernon, from him. 'We broke up two weeks ago.'

'No shit. You cheat?'

'Nah.'

'What, then?'

Brandon shrugged. They'd broken up because he was still moony over Callie. He and Natasha had been making out on the Harwich main beach in Cape Cod, and Brandon had accidentally called Natasha Callie by mistake. Oops. Natasha had climbed up the rickety wooden lifeguard stand and refused to come down until Brandon went away. Forever.

'Whose stuff is that?' Heath looked across the room and kicked his feet up on the brown tweed couch. There was a whole pile of bright pink canvas L. L. Bean bags that didn't have an owner yet.

Brandon shrugged. 'Don't know.' He picked up one of the tags. '"Jennifer Humphrey."'

'There's going to be a guy named Jennifer Humphrey in this dorm? Freaky.'

'No, *I'm* Jennifer.'

A little curly-haired girl in a sweet light purple Marc Jacobs knockoff skirt stood in the common-room doorway. Brandon knew the skirt was a knockoff, because he'd bought Natasha the real deal this summer. This Jennifer had a tiny upturned nose and pink cheeks and wore little skinny-heeled pink shoes with tiny cut-outs at the front so he could just glimpse her toes peeking through.

'Hi,' she said simply.

'Uh,' Brandon stammered. 'You're not . . . supposed to be—'

'No . . . actually . . . I am.' She laughed a little. 'I was assigned to this dorm.'

'So you're *Mister* Jennifer Humphrey?' Heath butted in, crossing one foot over the other.

'Yeah. Waverly had me down as a guy.'

Brandon had a pretty good idea what Heath was thinking right then: *With tits like those, you certainly don't look like a guy.* God, his friends annoyed him sometimes. 'I'm Brandon.' He offered his hand politely, stepping in front of Heath.

Jenny tugged at her skirt. 'Hello.' She felt a little flustered. Of the seven boys who were milling around the lounge with their stuff, she'd picked out the two cutest. Brandon was gorgeous, with his flawless skin, perfect dark gold hair, and long, luxurious eyelashes, but he was prettier than she was! Jenny liked boys who looked a bit rougher and messier, like the one sitting behind Brandon, whose dirty blond hair was slightly greasy and whose Kelly green oxford shirt looked slept in. She stared at him again, realizing that he was the boy who'd given her the ride up the hill. The one who was having the party. Didn't he recognize her?

'I'm just supposed to wait here until they figure out what to do with me.' She looked directly behind Brandon, trying to jog his hot friend's memory. 'Can I hang out with you?' She tried to keep her voice steady. *New Jenny does not squeak when inviting herself to hang out with hot boarding school boys!* she silently scolded herself, digging her nails into her palms.

'Sure,' the guy answered, staring directly at her chest.

'What are you doing here, anyway?' Jenny looked around. 'Does everyone have to hang out in the lobby before they get assigned rooms?'

'Nah, we're just screwups, so we're stuck here until they tell us where we can go.' He grinned, whipping a BlackBerry out of his khaki pants pocket.

Jenny sat down. 'What did you do wrong?'

'Don't listen to Heath.' Brandon shook his head. 'The Waverly teachers are just assholes.'

Jenny started discreetly wiping the mud off her pink

shoes as best she could. 'So I'm a little freaked out. Something totally attacked me on my way over here. It was like . . . a giant flying cat.'

'Ohhh . . . That's a great horned owl,' Brandon explained. 'They're all over the campus. Someone donated a pair of them like a hundred years ago and they spawned. But even though they practically kill kids all the time, the horned owl is our mascot. I guess it's, like, Waverly tradition to have them around.'

'They crap all over the place,' Heath added.

'Oh, I like traditions,' Jenny exclaimed quickly. 'But the thing swooped for me like it didn't want to miss!'

'How *could* it miss?' Heath muttered, typing on his BlackBerry. He looked straight at Jenny's boobs again. Old Jenny would have been embarrassed, she thought, but not New Jenny. She would call him out.

'Is there something wrong?' she asked politely, folding her hands in her lap.

Heath smiled wryly, then cocked his head. 'Wait a sec.' He stopped. 'You said you were from the city? As in, New York?'

'Yes. The Upper West Side.'

Heath's eyes lit up like a slot machine. 'Have you heard of a club called Hen Party?'

Jenny furrowed her eyebrows. 'No . . .'

'Maybe I'll take you some time.'

'Inappropriate,' Brandon muttered. Hen Party was some strip club in Manhattan everyone was suddenly talking about. He looked from Heath to the new girl. They seemed to be in some sort of force-field staring contest with each other. She looked smitten, but whatever. Heath might be Brandon's friend, but he was the human version of a Monet – he only looked good from afar. Close up, once you got to know him, he was pretty . . . well, ridiculous. *Just wait until you find out that he has a bad toenail-clipping habit*, Brandon thought, gritting his teeth. *Just wait until you find out he gossips more than a girl. Just wait until you find out the girls call him Pony behind his back, because everybody has taken a ride.*

The staring contest continued. Then a little high-pitched noise rang out, and Heath's attention quickly swerved back to his BlackBerry. Pop! Force field deactivated.

'*Mister* Jennifer Humphrey,' he muttered again, 'from the Upper West Side.' He tapped out a few more lines and threw his BlackBerry back into his bag. Then he stripped off his T-shirt and rubbed his golden-brown, summer-spent-in-Nantucket chiseled torso. 'I'm going to take a shower. Wanna come?'

Jenny opened her mouth to respond, but Heath wheeled around, found a fluffy white bath towel in his duffel bag, and sauntered off to the bathroom.

Brandon sighed and pulled out his silver Motorola Razr. He scrolled through a few e-mails – just some more welcome-back messages and speculative gossip about what had happened to Tinsley Carmichael. He could sense Jenny watching him and couldn't help but get all tingly.

'Are we allowed phones?' Jenny asked.

'Well, no. We can't talk on them. But everyone texts and IMs on their phones. You just log on to Owlnet and use your Waverly e-mail address, which is just your first and last name, no spaces. It's a loophole the faculty hasn't figured out yet.'

'Shoot. I didn't bring mine. The manual said no cell phones.'

'"Waverly Owls must not use cell phones on campus,"' Brandon recited in a mock-serious voice.

Jenny giggled. 'Yeah. I love all the Waverly Owls stuff.'

Brandon smiled. 'Apparently one of the old Waverly headmasters wrote the manual right after the Roaring Twenties, maybe during, like, Prohibition or something, when manners and good behavior were really important. I guess owls were the mascots back then, too. It's been adapted for modern times, with cell phones and stuff.'

'Funny.' Jenny felt herself relax a little. Her cheeks hurt from smiling so much already today.

'So there's a party in this lounge tonight. Maybe you wanna come?'

'A party?' Jenny raised her eyebrows eagerly. 'Sure.'

'I mean, it'll be pretty casual, but it's tradition, you know?' Brandon shrugged. He seemed less shy without Heath around.

Jenny bit her lip, which Brandon found irresistible. She was so fresh-faced and seemed so excited to be there, different from all the cookie-cutter, Fair Isle sweater, Gucci sunglasses, Barbie-goes-to-boarding-school Waverly girls who took it all for granted. Now if only she could stay off the Pony ride before classes even got started . . .

'Well,' Jenny interrupted his interior monologue. 'If it's

a tradition, then I'll have to come. Heath will be there too?'

Heath slunk through the lounge doorway. His shaggy blond hair was dripping water down his bare chest, and the white bath-towel was tied right under his chiseled hipbones. He wasn't holding anything except for his BlackBerry, and he smiled at it as he spoke. 'I wouldn't miss it.'

OwlNet   Instant Message Inbox

HeathFerro: I already met stripper girl. Twice.

RyanReynolds: ???

HeathFerro: Dad gave her a ride to the front office. Then me and Brandon were sitting in Richards and she came in. She plays it cool, though. Real innocent. But you can tell she's naughty.

RyanReynolds: She snuck into a boys' dorm already? Did she show you her thong?

HeathFerro: Not yet . . .

5

EVEN WHEN PROVOKED, A WAVERLY OWL SHOULD REMAIN CIVIL TO HER ROOMMATE.

'Mom, can you please tell Raoul that he doesn't have to come into the dorm with me? This is *embarrassing*.' Brett Messerschmidt tried to balance a cream-colored Chanel quilted purse and a black Jack Spade laptop bag in one hand and a giant Hermès shopping bag in the other while cradling her platinum Nokia against her shoulder. Her parents' personal assistant, Raoul, who was two hundred sixty pounds and bald, struggled to lift some of her seemingly endless luggage without ripping his black suit. Finally he gave up and took off his jacket, revealing a perspiration-stained white shirt and a mountain of muscles.

'Honey, you need his help,' her mother cooed in her

thick New Jersey accent on the other end of the line. 'You can't carry those heavy suitcases all by yourself!'

Brett groaned and slammed her phone shut. Everyone else carried their own stuff — no matter how loaded they were. Drivers just left their bags on the curb in front of the dorm. It wasn't as if anybody was going to walk off with your shit. But her parents, Stuart and Becki Messerschmidt of Rumson, New Jersey, babied her as though she were one of their shivering Teacup Chihuahuas.

Her parents — *shudder*. Her father, the most prominent plastic surgeon in the tri-state area, was known for bragging about the highest percentage of fat he could lipo out of a patient in a single sitting. And the only time Brett's mom had accompanied her to Waverly, when Brett was an eighth grader and touring the school, Mrs Messerschmidt had told a particularly WASPy-looking mother that her chin was just *perfect* and had asked who she used. The woman had stared at Mrs Messerschmidt blankly before finally getting it and storming away.

Ever since she'd started Waverly, Brett had straight-up lied about her parents. She claimed they lived on an East Hampton organic farm but summered in Newfoundland, that her father was a cardiologist and her mom threw small-scale Canadian charity events. She had no idea why that was the story she'd come up with, but anything was better than the real story, which was that her parents were nouveau riche and the tackiest people Brett had ever met. Everyone at Waverly bought it, except for Tinsley, who last year had answered Brett's cell phone when she wasn't in the room and had a lengthy conversation about leopard versus tiger prints with Mrs Messerschmidt, who was of course calling from her Rumson, New Jersey – not East Hampton – home. That was one good thing about Tinsley not coming back: at least her embarrassing parents would remain a secret.

'You really don't have to help me, after driving all this way.' Brett smiled apologetically at Raoul. She'd have to remember to send him some Kiehl's All-Sport Muscle Rub for when he got home.

'It's fine,' Raoul replied in his baritone voice, but Brett thought she detected a slight groan when he dropped her bags and headed back to get the next round from the car.

When she unlocked her dorm room door, her best friend, Callie, who had a perfect, *untacky* pedigree – her mother was Scarlett O'Hara incarnate and the governor of Georgia, for God's sake – smirked as Raoul fussed over exactly where Brett's oversize Louis Vuitton sweater trunk would go.

'Oh, wherever's fine!' Brett said quickly. Then she turned back to Callie. 'Hey.'

'Hey, yourself.' Callie leaned against the window and crossed her arms.

She looked like she'd spent the whole summer getting twisted and prodded by her Pilates instructor, Claude, and eating nothing but Trident gum. Her hair was shoved into a messy low ponytail, and she had that slightly dazed, you'd-think-she-was-ditzy-if-you-didn't-know-better look in her hazel eyes. A pale orange cotton skirt and top lay in a rumpled pile on the floor, and now she was wearing a faded baby-blue T-shirt, mini Ralph Lauren terry-cloth boy shorts, and gymnastics socks with little pink fuzzy balls at the heels.

Where Callie was cute and pretty in a preppy way – she was captain of the girls' field hockey team, after all – Brett was more unusual-looking. She had pale, milky-white skin and very red bob-length hair. Her green eyes were almond-shaped and both her nose and chin came to mischievous-looking points.

It was weird suddenly seeing Callie and comparing herself to her again. Last year, Brett, Callie, and Tinsley had been three peas in a pod. But then the E thing had happened and everything had changed. No one knew why Tinsley was the only one who'd been kicked out, but Callie had always had a particular talent for persuasion – freshman year, she'd convinced Sarah Mortimer to go out with Baylor Kenyon instead of Brandon Buchanan, all because Callie had wanted Brandon for herself. And last year, Benny Cunningham, their well-bred, beautiful brunette friend from Philadelphia, had wanted to go out with Erik Olssen, a pale, hot Swedish import, but he'd liked skanky Tricia Rieken – who'd had a boob job and wore the sluttiest, most dominatrixlike clothes from Dolce & Gabbana. Somehow Callie had managed to persuade Tricia to like Lon Baruzza, who was on scholarship but gorgeous and allegedly very good at sex, leaving Erik open for Benny.

Clearly Callie was good at getting people to do whatever she wanted, especially when she had something to gain personally. And in this case, maybe Callie was better off without Tinsley around: last spring, Tinsley and Callie's boyfriend, Easy Walsh, had been spotted by the girls' soccer team behind the row houses at night – alone. Both Tinsley and Easy had denied that anything had happened, but Callie could get pretty territorial when it came to boyfriends. It seemed crazy that Callie would get Tinsley kicked out of school for possibly hooking up with Easy, but, well, Callie was a little insane.

Callie squinted. 'Did your hair get redder?'

'Kind of,' Brett mumbled. Her colorist, Jacques, had fucked up and used a blue red on her instead of a yellow red. She'd gone to Bergdorf's to get it fixed but had managed to get the salon's most punk rock stylist, who had told her it was perfect and that it would go against his artistic sensibilities to change it. Brett worried that she looked too much like Kate Winslet in that *Eternal Sunshine* movie, which was *not* a good look.

'I like it,' Callie declared. 'It looks awesome.'

Liar! Brett knew what Callie thought of fake-looking dyed hair. Brett slammed her bag down on the floor. 'So what, you don't call me all summer?'

'I . . . I called you,' Callie stammered, widening her eyes.

'No, you didn't. You sent me one text message. In June.'

Callie stood up. 'Well, you didn't respond!'

'I . . .' Brett trailed off. Callie was right. She hadn't responded. 'So, did you hear from Tinsley?'

'Of course.'

Brett felt a stab of jealousy. 'Me too,' she lied. She hadn't heard from her glamorous best friend since she'd been expelled last May.

They both stared at Tinsley's bare bed. Would it be empty all year? Maybe they'd use it for extra storage or cover it with an Indian batik bedspread and embroidered pillows from one of the hippie Rhinecliff stores. Or would Waverly stick them with some weirdo no one wanted to room with?

'Tinsley called me a whole bunch of times,' Callie continued, a little aggressively.

'Me too,' Brett lied again, removing some of her blouses from her cream-colored leather suitcase. 'So, how's Easy?' She changed the subject. 'Did you see him this summer?'

'Um . . . yeah,' Callie replied quietly, a twinge of hurt in her voice. 'Did you see Jeremiah?'

'Yeah, some,' Brett mumbled back.

'Still hate the way he says *car*?' Callie asked as she examined her clear lip gloss in a tiny black lacquered Chanel compact.

'Yes,' Brett groaned. Her boyfriend, Jeremiah, was the star lineman for St Lucius and even though he was from an old-money family in Newton, a well-to-do suburb of Boston, he spoke with a Boston townie accent, omitting his *r*'s like Matt Damon in *Good Will Hunting*.

'Did you visit him or did he visit you?'

'Well, I spent a week with his family on Martha's Vineyard. That was really nice.' Brett liked Jeremiah, but she really loved his family. They were textbook New England wealthy – so understated and tasteful and the exact opposite of her trashy parents. It didn't hurt either that Jeremiah was gorgeous, with an angular, square jaw, floppy reddish-brown hair to his shoulders, and blue-green eyes that drank her in.

Brett had promised that, as soon as she got to school, she'd call him up and they'd have phone sex. Jeremiah had wanted to have sex over the summer, but she just wasn't ready. She wasn't entirely sure why, except that she'd never had sex with anybody before, and she really wasn't sure if Jeremiah was the right person to do it with first.

Of course, indecision about losing her virginity wasn't the kind of thing a girl like Brett ever admitted out loud. She'd told Callie she'd lost it ages ago to a Swiss boy named Gunther she'd met on a family skiing trip to Gstaad, even though really she'd hardly even let him feel her up. Brett had cultivated an image at Waverly: tough, experienced, sophisticated, and a little bitchy. Her mom was the opposite – helpless, naive, childish – and Brett didn't want to be like that.

Callie extended her long, perfectly smooth legs. 'I really need a shower.' She yawned, stood up, and slipped on a pair of rubbery clogs. 'You want to go to dinner when I get back?'

Brett shrugged. 'I don't know. I have to look over some prefect stuff for tomorrow. There's some new adviser, so I need to be prepared and stuff.' Brett had been elected junior prefect last year, which meant she would lead roll call and act as junior leader of DC, or Disciplinary Committee. It was a huge popularity nod – everyone in your class had to vote you into the position. 'But I guess I could skip it. And we have the party tonight, too . . .'

'Whatever.' Callie waved her towel and turned for the door.

Brett flopped onto her bed and stared out the window. The view of the river, which usually calmed her down like a shot of aged whiskey, now seemed suffocating. She'd imagined her first meeting with Callie after the long summer would be different. She hadn't expected them to talk about Tinsley right away, and she'd assumed Callie would behave like she used to – throwing herself on Brett's bed, opening a bag of Pirate's Booty for them to share, and gossiping about all the wild, romantic, risqué stuff they'd done all summer. They'd laugh, have some gin and tonics, and go to dinner, just like last year.

She flipped open her cell phone and quickly hit the shortcut key to call her sister, Brianna, who lived in New York and worked as a fashion editor at *Elle* magazine. Bree had been through the Waverly mill six years before and could usually talk Brett out of any funk. Unfortunately, Bree's phone went straight to voice mail.

'Hey, it's me,' Brett rambled when she heard the beep. 'I feel . . . I don't know. A mess. Call me or something.'

She hung up and flopped back on the bed. As soon as she did, her cell phone bleated in her bag. Thinking it was Bree, she opened it up, but she was wrong.

'Hello, Jeremiah,' she sighed, pressing the phone to her ear. 'How are you?'

'Wicked awesome, now,' he breathed on the other end.

Brett rolled her eyes. Then she pictured him spread-eagled on his St Lucius bed, ten miles away, in a tattered varsity football jersey and boxer shorts, with his long tan arms and sexy eyes, and she felt a warm whoosh of pleasure.

'So are we going to do this . . . thing?' she asked, not even bothering to shut the dorm-room door. Let the nosy sophomore girls next door get an earful. Maybe they'd learn something.

OwlNet Instant Message Inbox

HeathFerro: I got news. Talked to my older brother's friend who works in I-banking, and he says that this place Fish Stick is the bomb in the city. Girls take it off for 99 cents!

CallieVernon: Um, Heath? I think you got the wrong text addy. This is Callie. I don't want to hear about strippers. Especially not as I'm about to take a shower.

HeathFerro: You're in the shower? Can I see? Now that you and Easy are broken up, you're a free bird, right?

CallieVernon: What? Who told you that?

CallieVernon: Heath? Where are you? It's not true!

CallieVernon: Hello??

OwlNet   Instant Message Inbox

BennyCunningham: So the big question going around is, you take a ride on the pony yet?

CallieVernon: Pony?

BennyCunningham: It's the new name for Heath Ferro. He gets more ass than a pony at a country fair.

CallieVernon: Ew. No way have I hooked up with him. He's nasty. Have YOU?

BennyCunningham: Guilty as charged.

CallieVernon: OMG. When?

BennyCunningham: Freshman year. We made out in the Stansfield Hall coatroom. Never again. Totally gross.

CallieVernon: Not to change the subject, but has anyone told you Easy and I broke up?

BennyCunningham: Umm . . . maybe.

CallieVernon: Who?

BennyCunningham: Can't remember. Gotta go to predinner prep!

CallieVernon: Because it's not true.

CallieVernon: Seriously.

CallieVernon: U still there?

6

IF IT WILL IMPRESS HER ROOMMATES,
A WAVERLY OWL MAY DISH HER OWN DIRT.

'I'm looking for Jennifer Humphrey.' A thin, birdlike girl with a British accent and stringy blond hair stood twitching in front of Brandon and Jenny, just inside the door to Richards' lounge. She wore a plain white sleeveless cotton turtleneck with a little triangular crest over the pocket and very suburban-mom-looking khakis, the kind that cinch around your waist and make your ass look huge. 'I guess that would be you.'

'Yes,' Jenny half-squeaked, trying to keep the eagerness out of her voice.

'I'm Yvonne Stidder.' The girl stuck her hand out. She had a flimsy handshake and acne on her chin. 'I'm a mentor to new students. We found you a room.'

Brandon raised his eyebrows at Jenny and started to get up. 'It was nice meeting you, Jenny.'

'You too.' Jenny hefted her pink L.L. Bean duffels onto her shoulder. 'I'll see you tonight,' she whispered when Yvonne had turned her back.

'I'm so sorry we kept you waiting for so long,' Yvonne continued, leading Jenny down the Richards stairwell, past an entryway full of already-moved-in Trek mountain bikes, skateboards, empty PlayStation boxes, and about a dozen well-used soccer balls.

'No big deal.' Jenny was thrilled to have hung out with those two cool boys, but she was kind of relieved to be away from them, so she could breathe a little.

'Normally we aren't allowed in the boys' dorms except during visitation hours.' Yvonne gave Jenny a sidelong glance, holding the door open for her. She sneezed as soon as they stepped outside. 'Actually, um, that was the first time I've ever been in a boys' dorm. Although of course I know everything about the boys' dorms. I know all sorts of facts about Waverly if you want to ask me any questions. Anything at all.'

'Okay. Thanks.' If Yvonne hadn't seemed like such a dork, Jenny might've suspected she was coked up, she talked so fast. 'So what dorm am I in?' she asked as they crossed the green. She felt a nervous flutter in her chest. They were going to her new dorm, where she'd live for the whole school year! Where all sorts of amazing things would happen to her! Hopefully.

'Dumbarton. Over there, see?' Yvonne pointed to a two-story brick building with cutout windows sticking out of the roof at the back of the campus. Beyond it shimmered the Hudson, which looked a lot prettier up here than it did in the city. Jenny could just picture the boys' crew team gliding effortlessly across its surface in their sleek sculls, their strong arms bulging as they rowed. 'This girl Tinsley Carmichael – she was going to live with Callie Vernon and Brett Messerschmidt, but then she got kicked out, so there's a free spot. My friend from jazz ensemble, Storm Bathurst, lives next door—'

'Wait. Did you say Tinsley?' Jenny asked. She recognized that name, but she'd absorbed so much in so little time that she couldn't remember when or where. 'Why'd she get kicked out?'

Yvonne shoved her round, wire-rimmed glasses further up her nose. She smelled like Vicks VapoRub. 'I'm not sure,' she replied flatly. 'I don't like to gossip.'

'Well, can you tell me *anything* about my new roommates?'

Yvonne paused. 'I don't know them well. But they're the girls everyone flocks around.'

'Flocks around?' Jenny's heart sped up.

'You know, the ones always giving parties, always with the cutest boys . . .' Yvonne giggled and turned to Jenny. 'Not to say there aren't cute boys in the jazz ensemble. Do you play any instruments? The jazz ensemble is looking for some people.'

'Um, no, sorry. But about Callie and Brett – they're, like, really popular?'

'Yeah.' Yvonne nodded, sidestepping a maroon pinnie that someone had left on the field. 'There's this little crowd of kids that everyone on campus watches.'

Oh, really? Jenny thought excitedly. She touched the preppy little alligator on her shirt, pleased that she'd dressed so nicely to meet her supercool new roomies. Then she noticed a tall, brunette boy with matted hair, as if he'd just taken off a hat, walking across the green. He carried a big wooden easel over his shoulder, and his jeans were spattered with paint. Jenny's breath caught in her throat.

'Who is that?' She pointed.

'Him?' Yvonne muttered. 'That's Easy Walsh.'

'Easy. What a great name,' Jenny mused. 'Is he an artist or something?'

'I don't know him very well, except that he's always getting into trouble.' Yvonne crinkled her nose. 'Smoking,' she whispered. For a girl who didn't like to gossip, she certainly knew a lot.

The boy entered the double doors of the library. Jenny suddenly wished she could ditch her bags – and Yvonne – and follow him.

Instead, she followed Yvonne into the Dumbarton dorm. It was a quaint, two-story brick building that had its name inscribed in brownstone above a large, white, wooden farm-house door. They ducked through a narrow passage and up a set of granite stairs. One of the steps was inscribed 1832, RHINECLIFF, NY. The dorm was even older than Jenny's family's crumbling rent-stabilized apartment building on the Upper West Side.

All around her, girls were moving their things in. Rooney blared out of one room, No Doubt out of another. She saw a short Asian girl with pigtails unrolling a giant poster of Jennifer Garner as Elektra, kicking someone's ass.

They approached door 303, which was slightly ajar.

'. . . and I'm licking you all over, and – wait. No. Jesus, Jeremiah, you don't have your pants off yet. Stay with me here!'

'Uh, hello?' Yvonne said, pushing the door open a little.

A striking-looking older girl with blazing red hair sprang up from one of the room's twin beds. 'I have to go,' she blurted into her phone and flipped it shut. She glanced for a second at Yvonne and then fixed her piercing eyes on Jenny.

'Ermm, this is Jenny Humphrey,' Yvonne explained. 'She's your new roommate. She's from . . . where was it?'

'Constance Billard,' Jenny answered, sticking out her hand. 'In New York City.'

'Oh. Cool. Brett Messerschmidt.' The girl wore a starched, short-sleeved tailored white blouse that Jenny had seen in the windows of the Soho Scoop store all summer and those knee-length pegged shorts only the hippest kids in Williamsburg were wearing.

Jenny walked into the room, which was bigger and somehow plainer than she'd imagined. The windows were huge and beautiful, overlooking the river, while the beds and furniture were just . . . old. She studied her new roommate out of the corner of her eye. Her blazing red hair was cut in a severe bob that ended right at her chin. One ear had about seven tiny gold hoop earrings, and she wore a gold diamond Cartier tank watch on her left wrist. She was sexy and sophisticated, and very . . . familiar. Then Jenny remembered: there was a picture of Brett on Waverly's Web site. She was the Girl Hovering Over Her Books Looking Studious. Or at least that's what Jenny had called her.

'What about Callie?' Yvonne looked around the room. 'Is she here yet?'

'Shower,' Brett muttered.

Yvonne blinked furiously, then mumbled something about a flute lesson and fled the room.

Jenny walked over to what looked like the spare bed and sat down, bouncing a couple of times. 'This is a great room. I love the view.'

'Yeah, it's okay.' Brett folded her arms across her chest.

'Who are *you*?' came a loud voice behind them. Jenny turned and saw a tall, strikingly beautiful girl with enormous hazel eyes and dark blond hair that looked like it had just been blow-dried. Jenny thought she looked just like the Disney movie version of Cinderella. Once she had transformed into a princess, of course.

'Hey. I'm Jenny. I'm – they assigned me to this room.'

'They? Who's "they"?' Cinderella demanded.

'Well . . . Waverly,' Jenny stammered. 'Are you Callie?'

'Yes. Are you a junior or a sophomore?'

'Sophomore. What are you guys?'

'Juniors.' Callie pursed her pink-lipsticked lips and deposited an enormous Gucci makeup bag on top of her desk. 'You're taking that bed?' She pointed to the bed Jenny was sitting on.

'I guess so. I mean, unless it's not okay with you two.'

'I suppose it's fine.' Callie glanced at Brett. 'I guess Tinsley's really gone then.'

Brett made a snorting noise through her nose. Jenny just stood there, not sure what to say.

'What happened to . . . er . . . Tinsley?' she finally asked.

'It's complicated,' Brett responded quickly, unzipping a suitcase entirely full of shoes. Jenny checked the labels on a few. Jimmy Choo. Sigerson Morrison. Manolo Blahnik.

'It was nothing,' Callie added. She stared out the window, away from both of them.

Jenny wasn't much of a smoker, but she wished she could have a cigarette right then, just to have something to do with her hands.

Callie finally broke the silence. 'Where'd you go to school before this?'

'Constance Billard? It's in—'

'New York City. All girls,' Callie interrupted in a breathy voice, sliding a little closer to Jenny in the same way a cat might rub up against your calf. She turned to Brett. 'Didn't Tinsley go to Constance?'

'No. She went to Trinity. Until fifth grade. Then she went somewhere in Switzerland, then here.'

'Yeah, Tinsley definitely didn't go to an all-girls' school, now that I think about it.' Callie examined her cuticles. 'I remember her saying that she had tons of boyfriends.'

'Well, Tinsley's beautiful,' Brett added offhandedly, taking T-shirts out of another suitcase.

Jenny bristled. Was Brett saying that she wasn't beautiful? Who was this Tinsley girl, anyway?

'She could get any guy she wanted,' Brett continued. 'Even guys with girlfriends.'

'That's not true,' Callie snapped, before turning back to Jenny.

Jenny's eyes darted back and forth between her room-mates. What was up with them?

'Tinsley had her eleventh birthday party at Chelsea Piers. Like, she rented out the whole thing and installed a trapeze school in the gym area. Did you go to that?'

Jenny shrugged. 'Sorry, no.' But she remembered that party, all right. Back when she was ten, Jenny's father had ranted for days about an article in the *New York Times* Style section covering a party at the Chelsea Piers Sports Complex for a girl a year older than Jenny. Her dad had mocked it for being indulgent and piggishly bourgeois, but Jenny had thought the girl was the luckiest kid on the planet. And now she'd be sleeping in her bed! This *had* to be a good sign.

Callie looked at Jenny like a Christie's appraiser might examine a Ming vase and then smiled. 'Well, welcome to Waverly. I think you're going to like it here.'

Jenny hugged herself. *I like it already.*

OwlNet   Instant Message Inbox

TeagueWilliams: What did you say the 99-cent girl looks like?

HeathFerro: Brown curly hair, practically a midget, major knockers.

TeagueWilliams: So lemme guess . . . You taking her to the chapel?

HeathFerro: Hells yeah!

OwlNet   Instant Message Inbox

CelineColista: So Callie and Brett are pissed at each other. They're both going to Marymount's office to get a room transfer.

BennyCunningham: All 'cause of Tinsley, huh? Where is she, anyway? Does anyone even know?

CelineColista: I heard she's dating some guy from the Raves and they're on tour in Europe.

BennyCunningham: I thought that new girl from the city was dating the Raves . . .

CelineColista: Which one!?

BennyCunningham: All of them. The whole band.

CelineColista: Gross. Where'd you hear that?

BennyCunningham: I have my sources.

7

CHAPEL IS NOT AN APPROPRIATE PLACE
FOR YOUNG OWLS TO SOCIALIZE.

'Well, look who's here!'

Jenny stood outside Richards' lounge, re-applying her translucent pink lip gloss in the large, smoky, café-style hall mirror. She was wearing a scoop-neck, emerald-green APC top that was getting a teensy bit stretched out by her cumbersome breasts, and the highest tan leather heels she owned. She whipped her head around to find Heath Ferro, the boy from earlier with the BlackBerry and the great abs, standing in the doorway, an unlit cigar-ette in his hand. Tiny beads of sweat stood out on his fore-head, and his eyes had a glassy, tipsy look.

'Hey,' she answered brightly, wiping her hands off on the only pair of Seven jeans she owned, which happened to make her legs look slightly longer than tree-stump length. 'Is the party in there?'

'Indeed it is,' Heath replied gallantly. He looped his arm around Jenny's waist.

Jenny smiled. Heath seemed really happy to see her. And she was happy to see him, too. He wore a light blue untucked oxford shirt, army fatigue shorts, and no shoes. She liked his broad shoulders and floppy, I'm-a-prep-school-boy-through-and-through haircut. *Sort of the way Hamlet would look if he were a real person*, Jenny thought. All that princely Danish breeding, plus a flicker of wildness in his eye.

And Jenny liked wildness.

Heath pushed the heavy wooden lounge door open for her. Everyone froze. 'It's cool,' Heath announced, his hand brushing accidentally against Jenny's boob. 'It's just us.'

Jenny glanced around the room. Her first Waverly party! She could have been stuck back in the dorm playing checkers with Yvonne, but instead she was breaking the rules on her very first night at boarding school! She could immediately tell that it had a different feel to the parties she'd gone to back in New York – no one was fooling around in the guest bedroom and they didn't have to worry about parents arriving back early from Paris. Someone had dimmed the lights and lit a bunch of candles. Everyone looked like they'd just stepped out of a J.Crew catalog – they were all so *pretty*, with perfect, glowing skin and healthy, athletic bodies that came from mandatory year-round sports. Each person was more beautiful than the last. Everyone was holding large insulated coffee mugs, which was a little puzzling, until Jenny realized that the mugs contained alcohol.

Across the room, Brett sat on the scratched leather couch with Callie, their friend Benny Cunningham, and Sage Francis, who had been regaling them with tales of the fabulous African safari she'd gone on this summer. It didn't sound so great to Brett. Flies, malaria, and smelly wild animals. *Fun!* She gazed toward the doorway, saw her new roommate waltz in on Heath Ferro's arm, and immediately elbowed Benny hard in the ribs.

Benny was from Main Line Philadelphia, stood to inherit $200 million, and was pretty in a horsey way: tall and lithe, with long, thick brown hair and enormous brown eyes. She was a prude and always blamed it on where she grew up, as if Philly were a different planet where the girls drank whole milk and saved themselves for marriage. Benny always quoted a Diane Keaton line from an old Woody Allen movie, *Manhattan*: 'I'm from Philadelphia, and we don't do things like that *there*.' She didn't quite realize that the line was meant to be a joke. Despite her prudishness, she was also a major gossip who read *Page Six* religiously but acted like she knew it all first-hand.

'Looks like Heath's gone in for the kill,' Benny's best friend, Sage Francis, laughed, pointing. 'Guess he knew where he could get some.'

Brett shrugged. She couldn't imagine her naïve new roommate being a slut, but there *was* something seemingly sparkly and fresh about Jenny that might make her irresistible to, say, an entire indie rock band, which was the rumor going around campus. And she did have some kind of air of mystery about her, which reminded Brett of someone. Tinsley, perhaps?

'So are you guys really applying for room transfers?' Sage whispered, touching Brett on her bare shoulder.

'Room transfers?'

Sage fluttered her heavily glittered eyelids. She always overused eye glitter, because a hot French guy she'd met in St Barts during spring break the year before had told her that it made her eyes look huge and sexy. 'I thought you and Callie were ready to scratch each other's eyes out.'

'Well . . .' Brett trailed off. 'I wasn't planning on transferring . . .' She looked at her roommate. Callie was across the room talking intensely to Celine Colista, the other field hockey captain. They'd all played field hockey together since arriving at Waverly freshman year, but Brett had never taken it as seriously as the rest of the girls. Would Callie really transfer rooms behind Brett's back? Had it come to that? She turned back to her new roommate, who was standing in the doorway and gazing starry-eyed, as if she'd never been to a party before in her life.

Jenny was kind of overwhelmed – but in a good way. Heath returned, weaving a strong-smelling Waverly travel mug in front of her face. 'For you.'

'What's in it?' she asked, taking the mug with both hands.

'Does it matter?' He grinned and clumsily tipped the contents of his own mug down his throat.

Jenny put the mug to her lips. The strong, sour liquid tasted like beer mixed with rum. It gurgled down her windpipe, bringing tears to her eyes.

'Hey, there's Brandon!' she managed to gasp. Brandon stood by one of the giant windows, surrounded by three tiny girls with matching white-blond ponytails. When he saw Jenny across the room, his face brightened and he waved. She raised her hand to wave back, but Heath grabbed it and pulled her to his side.

'It's time for the new girl to do our little initiation ritual,' he said, smiling devilishly.

'What?' Jenny frowned. 'I haven't heard of any initiation rituals.'

'Then you haven't been talking to the right people.' Heath took another long drink from his mug, then set it on the ancient silver radiator. 'Come with me.' He led her to the door.

On the way out, a couple of guys gave him high fives. 'Where you goin', Pony?' one of them asked. Heath just raised his eyebrows. The guys started laughing and making whooping, whinnying noises.

'What's that all about?' Jenny asked, glancing back at the hooting boys.

'Who the hell knows?' Heath muttered, as he opened the heavy wooden door for Jenny.

'Who's Pony? You?'

'Shhh,' Heath interrupted. Jenny pursed her lips together, feeling a little uneasy. But this was boarding school. Magical Waverly land. She was safe here, wasn't she?

Outside, the night was pitch-black and dead quiet except for the sounds of some crickets left over from summer. Heath stopped in front of the Waverly chapel, the building next to Richards. The chapel was squat yet stately, with stained-glass windows and a heavy oak door.

'What are we—?' Jenny started. She hadn't been inside the chapel yet – she would be tomorrow morning, for roll call, announcements and prayers.

Heath stubbed his cigarette out against one of the front windowpanes. 'It's a tradition for new Waverly students to go into the chapel before school actually starts.'

'You're not going to lock me in or anything, are you?' Jenny asked in a wavering voice, not caring how Old Jenny she sounded.

''Course not.' Heath raised his eyebrows. 'I'm coming in with you.'

'Oh.' Jenny's heart was picking up speed. 'Okay, then.'

Heath pulled on the enormous oak door until it opened. The chapel's inside was lit only with a few candles. And it was as quiet as . . . well . . . a church.

'It's really nice in here,' Jenny whispered.

'Sit over here with me.' Heath patted a space on one of the dark wooden benches. In the candlelight, with his hands curled neatly in his lap and his hair slicked back, Jenny wondered if she'd misjudged Heath. Maybe he was actually really spiritual and sensitive.

She slid into the pew next to him. 'So this is the ritual, huh?'

'Ritual?' Heath looked at her cluelessly.

'You said that—' Jenny stopped. Of *course* there wasn't a ritual. It was a trick.

They were silent for a minute, listening to the wind

pressing up against the sides of the chapel. Then Heath placed his hand over hers.

'You were so beautiful this morning,' he whispered breathily, mixing up the b and m, so that he said *mootiful* and *borning*. 'Especially when my dad gave you a ride up the hill.'

'Oh,' Jenny answered, beaming. He *did* remember! 'Well, thanks.'

'You're from that all-girls school in New York, aren't you?'

'Yeah.' Had she said that this morning? She didn't think so.

'Did you get kicked out?'

'Not exactly.'

Then Heath lurched toward her. She thought he'd just lost his balance, but his mouth was suddenly all over her face, and his tongue was poking through her lips. Jenny's first reaction was to push him away, but tingles of pleasure began to run up her spine. Heath was an amazing kisser, maybe better than anyone else she'd ever kissed. She touched the nape of his neck, squeezed her eyes shut, and allowed herself to be swept away. The wooden bench made tiny aching creaks and groans. Their slurpy kissing noises rang against the alcove ceilings. His hand traced the outlines of her fingers but then quickly moved down her wrist to her forearm and finally up to her chest.

Jenny slid away from him, alarmed.

'Whatsa matter?' Heath smirked, his eyes flickering back and forth from one of her breasts to the other. He didn't look like a spiritual little angel anymore.

'Well . . . this is a little fast,' Jenny managed. 'That's all.'

'Come on,' Heath urged, his voice getting sleepier. 'Jenny from New York. Crazy Jenny.'

'I'm not all that crazy,' Jenny contradicted. She had a creepy feeling that Heath was quoting someone. What had people been saying about her? And where had they gotten their information?

Then suddenly Heath tipped over, laid his head on the bench, and began to quietly snore. Jenny stood up. Heath was wasted. She looked around the empty chapel, his snores echoing off the beamed ceilings.

All this made her feel very Old Jenny. She sighed and looked around at the dimly lit chapel. School didn't officially start until tomorrow, she resolved. New Jenny was just getting warmed up.

OwlNet   Email Inbox

To: EasyWalsh@waverly.edu
From: HeathFerro@waverly.edu
Date: Wednesday, September 4, 9:50 A.M.
Subject: Dude . . .

Ease,

Missed a fucking awesome party. Can't even remember the end,
except for this fresh little sophomore and me were really getting
along. I'm still in bed and I think I'm gonna stay here all day. Bet
you had a fucking awesome excuse for not being there. Was it
Tinsley? You saw her this summer, right?

Hey man, write back, 'cause we all think you're dead.

Later,

H

OwlNet   Email Inbox

To: BrettMesserschmidt@waverly.edu
From: JeremiahMortimer@stlucius.edu
Date: Wednesday, September 4, 10:01 A.M.
Subject: Better in person . . .

Hey, B. You got off the phone so fast. Just when we were getting
to the good part! I can't go another day without seeing you. I
know your classes start tomorrow, but you're done by 4, right?
How about I hop the shuttle and come over tomorrow afternoon?
Maybe we could spend a little time under that downy comforter of
yours . . .

A WAVERLY OWL SHOULD NOT DRINK WITH HER TEACHER – UNLESS IT'S SNAPPLE.

'Oof!' Brett slammed into a tall guy as she walked down Stansfield Hall's third-floor hallway. She'd been trying to kill a couple of minutes catching up on e-mails on her cell phone's tiny screen before meeting with some new teacher named Mr Dalton, who was supposed to be the new Disciplinary Committee adviser. Jeremiah's message had just popped up on the screen. 'Sorry,' she muttered to the person who'd bumped into her, without looking to see who it was.

'You better watch where you're going with that. It's Brett, right?'

She looked up. An unbelievably handsome boy with mussed dirty blond hair was standing in front of her. He looked like Prince William but taller, tanner, and better. He wore a slightly rumpled Savile Row-tailored small-check oxford shirt with the bottom two buttons buttoned incorrectly. Brett couldn't help but imagine him haphazardly throwing it on over his hard, muscular chest, as he climbed out of bed.

'I recognize you from the picture in your student file,' the boy went on. 'I'm Eric Dalton, the new DC adviser.'

Oops. This was no boy. 'Oh! Um. Hi, Mr Dalton,' Brett stammered, shoving her cell phone in her pocket. 'I'm, uh, sorry about that.' She held out her hand.

He shuffled a coffee mug – the same maroon-and-white Waverly Owls mug that they mixed drinks in at their dorm parties – from one hand to the other and gripped hers. Brett was suddenly glad that she had a moisturizing fetish and that her palm would feel silky in his hand.

'Those aren't allowed here, you know.' Mr Dalton raised his eyebrows at her phone. For a second Brett thought he was serious and started to muster up an excuse. Then he whispered, 'But I won't tell . . . this time. Go sit down in my office and I'll be with you in a sec.'

Flustered, Brett smiled, wishing she had something witty to say.

The door to his office stood open. She walked in and looked around. For a guy who'd just arrived at Waverly, he sure had a lot of stuff. There were posters wrapped in brown paper on the floor, a large black globe that still showed Russia as the USSR, and books and papers everywhere. She noticed a decanter filled with what looked like red wine on the oak table in the corner, and her mind started to race.

Settle down, she told herself. *You're here because he's new to Waverly and he wants to meet all the DC members. That's probably cran-raspberry Snapple, not wine.*

She walked up to one of the posters that Mr Dalton had hung in a heavy, gilded frame. It was actually an old inscribed scroll, mounted and framed. She squinted at the Ancient Greek words and murmured, '"Praise each god as though they were listening."'

'How'd you know that?' a voice called out behind her.

Brett jumped. Mr Dalton stood in the doorway, grinning at her slyly, as if he knew a big secret and was ready to spill it. 'I spent a little time in Greece,' she said uncertainly.

'You want to sit down?' he asked. 'Sorry for all the papers.' He quickly picked a stack of papers up off a chair, leaning so close to Brett that she couldn't help but notice how good he smelled. Like Acqua di Parma, which was the only type of cologne she could stand on a guy.

'Can I get you anything?' Mr Dalton sat down in his high-backed brown leather chair. It made a farting creak, which both of them pretended not to notice. 'I have little fridge, some glasses, although I only have . . . well . . . actually, all I have, I think, is some pinot noir.' He frowned, then blinked hard. 'Sorry. I mean, obviously we can't have pinot noir. I don't know what that's even *doing* in here, because I wasn't drinking it or anything.'

Methinks Mr Dalton doth protest too much, Brett thought wryly, watching him nervously pull his shirt collar away from his neck. 'I'm fine,' she stated primly instead, perching on the edge of her chair.

Dalton switched on the flat-screen Mac G5 sitting on top of his desk. 'Okay. Brett. So they're making me put all the old DC cases into a database. They gave me the grunt-work jobs because I'm new.' He flashed his perfect teeth nervously, and she wondered silently if he just had amazing dental genes or if these were veneers. It was a tough call, one she wouldn't mind investigating more closely. With, say, her lips.

He shuffled the papers. 'So besides meeting all the DC appointees, I'm looking for someone to help me weed through all this DC stuff to get to the pertinent information and then help enter it into the computer. But it has to be someone who was on DC last year, because the material is confidential to non-DC students. Were you on DC last year?'

Brett licked her lips. 'Well, no,' she answered, wanting to lie.

'Oh.' Mr Dalton sounded disappointed. He let out a sigh. 'That's too bad.'

'We wouldn't have to tell anybody, though, would we?' Brett suggested slowly. 'I mean, I want to help. It would . . . it would look good on my transcript.'

Sure. That's why I want to do it, she thought. *My transcript.*

'I don't know . . .' Mr Dalton shook his head. He stared at her quizzically. Brett nervously brushed a hair off her cheek. 'How old are you?' he finally said.

'Seventeen.'

'Huh.' He tilted his head and smiled with one side of his mouth.

'What?'

'Well. You don't look seventeen. That's all.'

Guys said this to Brett all the time. They were always astounded she was still in high school. 'How old are *you*?'

He straightened up a little. 'Twenty-three. I just finished Brown.'

Brett unconsciously chewed the Hard Candy Vinyl polish off her pinkie.

'I'm going to go to grad school, but since I went to Waverly, I thought I'd pay my dues and teach here for a couple years,' Mr Dalton continued.

'I want to go to Brown,' Brett blurted out.

'I could imagine you there.' He nodded.

She stared at her gorgeous twenty-three-year-old teacher and didn't pull her eyes away for the second he stared back.

'All right.' He finally broke the silence. 'I think maybe we could figure out a way for you to help me – I mean, if you really want to.'

I want to, Brett wanted to say. *I really, really want to.* But she remained silent.

'Maybe we could meet up again tomorrow morning, before class? Oh, and the name Mr Dalton sounds really weird. Maybe I'll be used to it when I'm fifty and running the family business. But for now . . .' He lowered his eyes and then looked back up at her from beneath his thick blond lashes. 'Call me Eric?'

'Sure,' Brett agreed, smiling. She could think of a lot of things she'd like to call him.

Just then the papers that he'd removed from her chair started to slide off his desk toward Brett's lap. He lunged forward, grabbing for them. At the same time, Brett leaned down to catch some papers that had landed on the floor. Their heads collided.

Ouch. 'Fuck!' Brett cried, seeing a brief flash of white. Then she clamped her mouth shut. Even though most Waverly kids had dirty mouths, you weren't supposed to swear in front of the teachers. Waverly Owls must always have good manners, and bad language was a sign of indecency and bad breeding.

He rubbed his forehead, wincing. 'You okay?'

Brett swallowed hard. What if Mr Dalton thought she was uncouth and trashy? But then she noticed his concerned expression and decided he didn't care.

'I think I'll live,' she replied finally.

'Well, that's good,' he laughed. 'Because I'd definitely like to keep you alive.'

OwlNet

To: BriannaMesserschmidt@elle.com
From: BrettMesserschmidt@waverly.edu
Date: Wednesday, September 4, 10:53 A.M.
Subject: Hot, hot, hot

Hey Sis,

I just met the perfect guy. He's smart, gorgeous, shy, and sweet and hotter than the models in the Ralph Lauren Romance ads. Trouble, though: he's a teacher. As in, the kind that gives you homework assignments. The kind that sits up on the Waverly stage during assembly. The kind that grades papers and isn't supposed to touch students . . . I'm sure you get the gist. What to do?

xoxoxo,

Little Sis

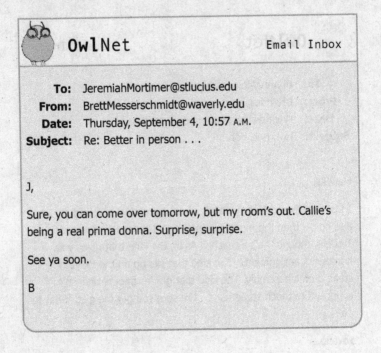

OwlNet

Email Inbox

To: JeremiahMortimer@stlucius.edu
From: BrettMesserschmidt@waverly.edu
Date: Thursday, September 4, 10:57 A.M.
Subject: Re: Better in person . . .

J,

Sure, you can come over tomorrow, but my room's out. Callie's being a real prima donna. Surprise, surprise.

See ya soon.

B

9

A WAVERLY OWL SHOULDN'T ATTEMPT SECRET TRYSTS. SOMEONE IS ALWAYS WATCHING.

Callie leaned up against the dusty wooden doors of the old stables, trying not to get dried horse manure on the heels of her brand-new Stella McCartney round-toed black patent leather shoes. The weathered red barn sat next to a three-acre horse paddock, separated from the rest of the Waverly campus by a patch of densely settled pines. A whistle blew in the distance, and Callie recognized the gruff voice of Coach Smail, the girls' field hockey coach, yelling, 'That won't cut it on varsity, ladies!' The first full day at school consisted of grueling eight-hour tryouts for the fall teams, but Callie was exempt since she was already a varsity field hockey captain.

The sun was low in the late-afternoon sky and Easy was walking toward her. He was wearing one of the T-shirts he'd taken home from her house – a ratty green thing with a horseshoe, of course – under his beat-up maroon Waverly jacket. No tie. His dark brown hair stood up in disheveled peaks and there was a smudge of blue ink next to his left ear. A huge, sexy smile spread across his face when he saw her. She wanted him so badly. Maybe everything between them was okay after all.

'You could've at least changed your shirt,' she teased, taking the hem between her fingers.

'I suppose, because I feel way underdressed next to you,' he teased back.

'I'm not all that dressed up.'

'Are too. Look at those shoes.' He pointed. 'I can imagine you standing in front of your closet, agonizing over your newest, sexiest pair. Right?' He smiled at her. 'I'm right, aren't I?'

'Wrong,' Callie shot back, although he was, of course, right. It pissed her off that Easy knew her so well. And that he was smarter than she was. Actually, when it came down to it, everything about him made her simultaneously seethe and shudder with pleasure.

Easy lit a cigarette and ducked so that he was out of sight of Marymount's house, a grand Tudor mansion right on the edge of campus. Callie tossed her long strawberry-blond hair behind her shoulders. Why was he just standing there? Here they were, alone by the abandoned horse stables, while everyone else was finishing up sports tryouts. She could hardly wait to lie down in the tick-infested hay and tear his clothes off.

'Missed you at the party last night,' she whispered tenderly.

'Mmm. Yeah. I was really tired.'

Okay, this was infuriating. He was *still* just standing there.

'So, you want to come over here?' Callie finally asked, pulling at his jacket.

'Just a sec.' He jerked away slightly and took another drag.

'Never mind, then. Forget it.' Callie backed away, pulling out her own pack of Marlboro Lights. She stuck one in her mouth and tried to flick on her fluorescent green lighter but kept fumbling with the childproof lock.

'No, no, come on,' Easy pleaded in a low voice, turning to her and throwing his cigarette on the ground. 'Don't be like that . . .'

'Well, I don't know,' Callie started. 'I mean, you—'

Easy put his hand on the nape of her neck. 'I'm just a little out of it.' He kissed Callie's jawbone lightly, then pressed her against the stable door and kissed her harder. His capable hands floated all over her body. Callie pulled a mess of tangled hair back from her face.

'Have I told you how good it is to see you?' Easy murmured between kisses.

Callie sighed. Things were suddenly right again. What had she been agonizing about? She and Easy were perfect together. Maybe she shouldn't have felt so freaked about what had happened in Spain. Maybe she shouldn't have paid any attention to that stupid IM she'd gotten from Heath saying they'd broken up.

'Maybe we could lie down?' she whispered.

Easy tugged her toward the paddock where the grass was green and soft, kissing her collarbone lightly. He pulled her to the ground and kissed her neck. *This is the way it should be*, she thought, looking toward the setting sun. The abandoned stables were beautiful and the sun was low and glowing pink in the sky. No, there wasn't any John Mayer playing softly in the background like there had been that night in Spain, but this would definitely do.

'D'you remember what we were talking about in Spain?' Callie murmured, her heart shivering in her chest. The memory of that night came rushing back: they had been in her bed, under the sheets, almost naked. Callie had mustered up all her courage and said to her beautiful, messy, sexy, brilliant, belligerent boyfriend, 'I love you.' She'd planned on having sex with him then: they'd tell each other they loved one other and then make love for the first time. All of the rumors about Tinsley from last year would clear up, and Easy would be hers forever.

Instead, he'd kissed her silently back, and then eventually the kissing had slowed, and he'd settled into the pillow next to her and fallen asleep. She'd listened to his breathing turn to soft snoring and wondered if he'd heard her at all. Maybe she'd said it too quietly? Callie had spent the whole summer hoping that was why he hadn't said it back.

Callie did love him, she really did. *Didn't he love her too?*

She noticed one of those fat great horned owls watching them from a tree branch. He looked like that stupid cartoon from those old Tootsie Roll commercials. She felt self-conscious, like the owl was judging her.

'Remember what I said in bed?' she asked tentatively.

Easy suddenly stopped kissing her collarbone and slumped against her side.

She touched his arm. 'What's wrong?'

'Nothing.' He breathed in deeply and looked out over the horse paddock. Shouts of the girls' field hockey tryouts echoed from the practice fields. 'This just seems . . . I don't know.'

'What do you mean?' Callie's voice came out in a high, embarrassing squeak. She shoved her Stella McCartney back on her right foot and sat up. A huge smear of gray dirt ran down her leg and she prayed it wasn't horse manure.

A male figure appeared on the path leading down to the stables, pushing a wheelbarrow.

'Shit.' Callie grabbed Easy's hands, pulling him up. 'It's Ben.'

Ben was the nasty old groundskeeper who always got kids in trouble. He even carried around a digital camera so he could have proof. Last year, he'd caught Heath Ferro smoking a joint by the natatorium, but Heath had bribed him to delete the photos by giving him his dad's platinum heirloom Harry Winston cuff links.

They scrambled to the other side of the stable and pressed themselves against a wooden door. 'I should probably go back to my room,' Easy whispered.

'Whatever.' Callie dug her heel into the dirt, even though she knew it was going to totally ruin her shoes. Shit. Why had she brought up Spain?

'Look.' He took her hands. 'I'm sorry. Let's try this again. Your dorm room. Tonight. After the welcome dinner.'

'Yeah, right,' Callie scoffed. 'You're already on Angelica's watch list.'

'I'll find a way.' Easy pulled her close and held her for a second. 'I promise,' he whispered, then dashed away.

OwlNet   Instant Message Inbox

AlanStGirard: Where's Heath?

BrandonBuchanan: Still in bed. Hasn't showered. Smells awful.

AlanStGirard: Dude, it's almost dinner!

BrandonBuchanan: I know. I think he's still drunk tho.

AlanStGirard: He left with that new chick last night.

BrandonBuchanan: Who?

AlanStGirard: Dark curly hair? Big boobs? They say she was a stripper in NYC.

BrandonBuchanan: Nah. She never showed last night.

AlanStGirard: Sure she did. You were too busy staring at Callie to notice. Heath took her to the chapel. Think she gave him a lap dance?

OwlNet	Instant Message Inbox

AlisonQuentin: This chapel stinks. Why is Marymount's Welcome to Waverly speech always so loooong?

BennyCunningham: No kidding. Where's u-know-who?

AlisonQuentin: Dunno. But did you know Sage drew a little pony on the marker boards of all the girls in her dorm who've hooked up with him? So far there are six, including the new girl. That's just one floor of Dumbarton.

BennyCunningham: How come I don't have a pony on my board?

AlisonQuentin: You hooked up w/ him?

BennyCunningham: We kissed freshman year! A little sloppy, but good technique.

AlisonQuentin: B! I thought you were my innocent friend!

10

THERE ARE SOME THINGS A WAVERLY OWL
DOES NOT EAT, JUST BECAUSE.

'You are part of a grand tradition.' The deep, penetrating voice of Dean Marymount boomed and thudded around the chapel. Everyone said Marymount had been this big revolutionary protester back in the seventies and that he was a card-carrying member of Mensa, but Jenny thought he looked more like a Little League coach who drove a Dodge minivan than the dean of a prestigious boarding school. His graying comb-over was plastered to his sweaty head. Behind him sat the Waverly faculty, all wearing the school's uniform – maroon and navy tie, maroon jacket, white shirt, trousers. Normally students just had to wear the maroon Waverly blazer with anything they wanted underneath, but for the first chapel meeting of the year everyone had to wear a tie, girls included. Jenny's half-Windsor knot was all lumpy. She sighed. Her father only owned one tie, which was covered in cobwebs. She'd never asked, but he'd probably had it since *he* was a sopho-more in high school.

They had gathered for Dean Marymount's official begin-ning-of-the-year speech before the first official all-campus dinner. The chapel was packed and smelled of teenaged-boy BO and feet.

Last night, she'd awakened Heath enough to deposit him on the stoop in front of Richards, and then she'd crawled back to Dumbarton, exhausted. In the middle of the night, either Brett or Callie had unplugged Jenny's clock radio to use the outlet to charge a cell phone. Luckily the chapel bells had woken her so she could get to field hockey tryouts on time. Every Waverly student had to play a sport, and Jenny had decided on field hockey, since it seemed like the most trad-itional boarding school sport to play. She planned on playing lacrosse in the spring for the same reason. Jenny didn't even have a hockey stick, but the bulldoggish coach, Alice Smail, had found her an extra Cranberry in the field house, and Jenny had soon discovered that she was a natural on the field.

'You're *sure* you didn't play for your school?' Coach Smail asked her. As if Jenny could have forgotten. Her scrimmage team's center, Kenleigh, whom Jenny had seen at the party last night, murmured, 'Good move,' as Jenny trotted back to the sidelines. Maybe she'd even make the varsity cut!

'This year, we have some new faculty members that I would like to introduce,' Dean Marymount announced. Jenny checked her watch. They'd already been here for forty minutes, singing Waverly's school hymn and Waverly's sports hymn, reciting the Waverly prayer to St Francis, and clapping as Marymount introduced the school's prefects, who were like the presidents of each class. Jenny was starving. 'First off, a Waverly alum and a recent graduate of Brown University, we have Mr Eric Dalton. Mr Dalton will be the new junior and senior ancient history professor and an adviser to the Disciplinary Committee. He's also the new assistant coach for the boys' crew team. Welcome.' Everyone clapped obediently.

Jenny spied Brett, who had just been forced to stand and wave at the class because she was the junior class's prefect, two rows ahead. Jenny watched as Brett elbowed the brunette next to her and mouthed the words *Oh my God*.

'I'd like to extend a warm welcome to all the incoming freshmen and new students — Waverly is your new home, and we are your new family,' Marymount continued. 'And finally . . . enjoy dinner!'

The crowd erupted in applause and hoots as it poured out of the chapel and across the great lawn toward the dining hall. Jenny gasped when she walked in. The dining hall looked like the inside of an old English cathedral. The walls were plastered with class pictures dating back to 1903 and with a lot of photographs of Maximilian Waverly, the school's founder.

Students milled around, kissing each other and slapping each other's hands. Jenny wasn't sure what to do. Where was she supposed to sit?

'It's a little crazy in here, huh?'

Jenny turned, hoping it might be Heath finally making

an appearance. Instead, standing next to her, was the boy
with the easel she'd seen across the green yesterday with
Yvonne. Easy. At least, that was what she thought Yvonne
had said his name was.

His hair was so brown it was almost black, and his eyes
were deep blue. He wore a beat-up green T-shirt with a yellow
silhouette of a horseshoe underneath his Waverly blazer. It
was the sort of chic T-shirt that they'd sell at Barneys for
$65, but his looked decidedly real-deal vintage. He voice was
gravelly, with an accent she couldn't quite place.

'A little crazy, yeah,' Jenny agreed. She stepped aside to
let him pass. A Smythson of Bond Street sketchbook hung
out of his green canvas messenger bag. A single sheet of
paper of sketched eyes, noses and mouths was clipped to
the cover. 'Hey, are you taking portraiture?'

'Yeah, I am. You?'

'Oh. Um, I am too.' Silently, Jenny attempted to pull
herself together. You're New Jenny now, she reminded
herself.

'Cool.' Easy slapped hands with a boy who'd just walked
in. 'So, see you later.' He smiled at Jenny.

'Hey,' a familiar voice beckoned from behind her. She
turned and smiled at Brandon, who looked even cuter and
cleaner than yesterday – if that was possible – in his maroon
Waverly blazer and striped tie. 'It's formal dinner. They
have assigned seating. You're at my table.'

'Oh. Thanks.' Jenny smiled gratefully and followed him
through the crowded dining room. 'So, um, how long did
the party go on last night?'

'Oh, the usual.' Brandon's eyes shifted to the floor. 'I didn't even see you there. Go home early?'

Jenny bit her lower lip. 'Um, yeah.'

They arrived at a table already occupied by two students: a very tall boy with a nose ring and a very tall girl whose angular face, large, wide-set brown eyes and thick brown hair all screamed good breeding.

'This is Ryan Reynolds, and this is Benny Cunningham.'

'I saw you at the party last night. I'm Jenny.' She smiled at Benny.

'That's right.' Benny nodded, shooting a knowing look at Ryan.

Jenny took off her hot wool Waverly jacket and draped it over her chair.

'You can't do that,' Benny hissed. 'The faculty will freak.'

'Oh.' Jenny quickly slid the jacket back on. She looked around the room; most of the students were sitting at their tables already, blazers on.

'Looking for Heath?' Benny blurted out. Ryan nudged her.

'Oh.' Jenny shook out her pristine maroon cloth napkin, hoping her face wasn't turning the same color. 'Yeah. He was . . . he was a little . . . tired last night. I had to help him home.'

'Bombed is more like it,' Ryan laughed. 'Anyway, Brandon, you getting psyched for Black Saturday?' he asked, stabbing the old wooden table with his knife.

'What's Black Saturday?' Jenny asked curiously.

'Don't get too excited,' Brandon laughed. 'It's when all

the St Lucius sports teams come to Waverly and we have this blowout bloodfest. The teams take it really seriously, because we're supposed to hate St Lucius so much. It's another tradition. You're playing field hockey, right?'

'Yes.' Jenny smiled. She'd never been on a team before. 'Tryouts were today.'

'Well, the girls' field hockey team plays, along with the soccer and football teams. But then when it's over, the kids from both schools party like rock stars at a secret location that isn't revealed until that day.'

'Heath usually throws the party,' Benny offered, refastening her silver Tiffany charm bracelet on her wrist. 'But maybe he told you that already?'

Student servers in starched white oxfords and pressed gray flannel trousers set down large, creamy white plates laden with grilled salmon marinated in honey wasabi. This was way better than her dad's experimental lamb-and-pineapple lasagna vodka flambé.

'Oh my God. This smells *delicious*.' Jenny grabbed her fork and took a huge bite. '*Mmm!*'

'Dude, you're eating the salmon?'

A boy put his elbows on the table next to her. Heath. *Finally*. 'Hey.' She covered her full mouth with her hand.

'Nobody eats the salmon,' Heath scoffed. There wasn't a hint of the amorous, you're-a-sex-goddess vibe he'd laid on last night.

Jenny's eyes widened. She looked around at the other plates, and sure enough, no one else at the table had touched their fish. 'Why? Is there something wrong with it?'

Brandon turned to her. 'No – it's fine. People just . . . don't eat it. I don't know why. It's like, a *thing*.'

'Jenny?' Someone tapped her on the back. She turned to see Yvonne, the girl who had escorted her to Dumbarton yesterday. Tortoiseshell butterfly clips held clumps of Yvonne's dishwater-blond hair back, and her pale blue eyes were as googly and crazed as they'd been yesterday. 'Can I talk to you?' Yvonne glanced nervously at the others at the table. 'In the hall?'

Ryan and Benny exchanged another knowing look. Jenny shrugged and placed her napkin over her fish. *New Jenny is not easily flustered*, she told herself. So what if no one ate the fish? New Jenny did what she pleased!

Yvonne led Jenny out into the front entryway of the dining hall.

'I hope this isn't about jazz ensemble,' Jenny declared up front. 'Because I'm kind of really not interested. I'm basically tone-deaf.'

'No, it's not that. I've, um, heard some things about you, and I thought you should know.'

'Huh?' Jenny sucked in her breath. She'd gotten I-thought-you-should-know speeches before, and it almost always turned out that she never wanted to know.

'Everyone's IMing about you.'

'What?' Jenny demanded slowly.

Yvonne took a deep breath. 'They're saying that you used to be a stripper and took your clothes off for, like, a dollar. And you're like this New York City sex legend. And, er, you've already slept with someone here at Waverly.'

'What!?' Jenny squeaked. Suddenly the hallway seemed dim and hazy. 'With whom!? I mean, who's saying that?'

Yvonne looked down. 'That boy who was at your table. Heath Ferro. I don't know if you even know him yet, but he—'

Jenny saw a red mist before her eyes. Heath. 'I can't believe this.'

'*I* don't believe it,' Yvonne protested, waving her hand around.

'Thanks,' Jenny squeaked.

'I have to go now. Sorry.' Yvonne turned and skittered out the door.

Jenny leaned against the wall, feeling dizzy and disoriented. *Heath.* Her entire body shook with horror and anger. Had Heath ruined her boarding school career before it had even started?

Brandon appeared in the arched doorway, frowning at her in concern.

'You okay?'

'I have to . . .' Jenny whirled around before she could finish her sentence, fleeing the dining hall. She sprinted across the damp green lawns, wishing she could take off and fly away like one of those fat old great horned owls. The ancient buildings of Waverly towered on either side of her, their windows glowering. The bite of salmon rebelled in her stomach, and Jenny slowed to a walk. She'd wanted to come to boarding school to start afresh, to become the girl she'd always wanted to be, to be a fabulous new, better version of herself. It was going to be a lot harder than she'd thought.

OwlNet   Instant Message Inbox

EasyWalsh: I'm right outside. Wanna check if the coast is clear?

CallieVernon: Hold on.

CallieVernon: OK, I just pressed my ear to Angelica's door, and I hear the TV. Loud. Looks good.

EasyWalsh: Cool. C u in a sec.

ONE GOOD WAY TO GET TO KNOW A WAVERLY OWL: FIND OUT WHAT COLOR J.CREW BOXERS HE WEARS.

'You *stink.*'

Jenny woke with a start. Where was she?

Oh, right. Waverly. In her room.

'I mean seriously, you really stink. Are you drunk?' someone whispered.

Was that Callie, talking in her sleep? Jenny had heard her come in: thankfully, it had been after she'd stopped sobbing into her pillow. She'd taken her clothes off in the dark, said 'nighty-night', and snuggled under the covers.

'I'm not drunk,' another voice slurred. A guy's voice.

'Well, you stink like vodka. Ew.'

'I love it when you say I smell,' the guy said.

'Shh. Pardee will hear.'

Jenny inched further beneath her covers. The voice sounded vaguely familiar. And whoever it was did stink — Jenny could smell something vaguely alcoholic, even though the windows were wide open and the cool night breeze was wafting though the room.

'Well, it would be nice, Easy, if you *didn't* stink, 'cause then I wouldn't have to taste it in your mouth.'

Easy?

Jenny's stomach dropped. How many Easys went to this school?

'You sure nobody's here?' he asked.

'Do you see anybody here?' Callie hissed.

Jenny stayed curled in a ball. Callie had seen her. She'd even said good night to her! Jenny wanted to leave them alone, but getting up and making noise right now would be very uncool. And what if Easy saw her? She was sure her crush on him would shine right through her, like her face was a mesh field hockey pinnie. To think that she had developed an immediate crush on her roommate's boyfriend! Old Jenny strikes again.

Her eyes adjusted to the dark and she peeked out from under the covers. Callie's bed was less than four feet away. There was a flash of naked skin in the moonlight. 'Condom,' Jenny head Callie whisper.

A pause. Then Easy's voice. 'Serious? Where?'

'Top drawer.'

Jenny heard fumbling in the dark. Then a scuffling of covers, and *thump*! Easy was halfway on the floor. He tried to get his balance but held on to the night table and ended up dragging it down with him. It made a horrible amount of noise. A box of Lifestyles Extra Lubricated condoms spilled out, along with a big bottle of Lubriderm dry skin lotion and a package of blue fine-tip Bic pens.

Jenny shot up in bed, staring at Easy's sprawled, naked body.

'Yo,' Easy drawled, grinning up at her. 'I know you.'

'Eep!' Jenny slunk back under the covers.

'Callie, you said nobody was here,' Easy whispered loudly.

Callie kicked the mattress angrily. 'This is ridiculous,' she sighed, and got out of bed. Jenny peeked out from under the covers and saw the outline of Callie's lithe body. She wore a pink bra with a pointy-toothed Lacoste alligator emblazoned on the strap. Where was Brett, anyway? Callie glanced over at the lump that was Jenny under the blankets. 'Sorry, Jenny.' She shrugged, then stomped over Easy, stepping on his hand as she headed for the door.

'Oww!' He cried out in pain. 'Where are you going?'

'Bathroom.' Callie flung the door open, and the room grew bright with fluorescent hallway light. Jenny buried herself deeper under the covers, mortified. *She's leaving us alone?* she wondered, horrified.

She heard Easy sit up, crack his neck, then sniff. 'So, is Jenny short for Jennifer?'

'Well, yeah,' Jenny croaked, still huddled under the covers.

'Didn't mean to make you so uncomfortable, Jenny,' he continued.

'Not a problem,' she murmured into her pillow. It smelled dusty and warm, like her Upper West Side home. She was glad she'd brought it, but it suddenly made her feel so homesick that she nearly burst into tears.

'You can stop hiding. I'm decent.'

Jenny peeped over the blanket with one eye. Easy had put his underwear back on, but that was all. His stomach was flat and muscular. And his boxers had a sailboat pattern she remembered from the J.Crew catalog. She wrenched her eyes away.

It was stiflingly hot under the covers. She sat up a bit, hoping that Callie would come back any second and take Easy someplace else so that he wouldn't have time to take in Jenny's swollen eyes and bed-head. She couldn't even imagine what she must look like right now, especially compared to Callie.

But apparently Easy didn't mind. He got off the floor and sat down on the edge of Jenny's bed. If she hadn't been completely stunned, she might have made room. But instead she stayed still. He was pressed right up against her.

'I was wondering when I'd get to meet you properly,' he mumbled, so quietly that Jenny could barely hear.

'What?' Jenny asked, even though she'd heard him fine.

'Nothing.' Easy looked up. 'Oh. The Seven Sisters.'

'What?'

'The constellation.' Easy pointed to the crusty old glow-in-the-dark stars someone had stuck to the ceiling years ago.

'Although to the naked eye there are only six stars easily visible.'

'Huh.' Jenny didn't know how to respond – not only to what Easy had just said but to this situation, *period*. Her dream crush was sitting on her bed. Old Jenny was totally horrified. New Jenny was practically quivering. Blended together, both Jennys were immobile and tongue-tied.

She looked at the outline of Easy's long, athletic-looking feet. His second toes were longer than his first. What was that a sign of again? Wait. *Hello*? Was that his hand on her back?

Okay. This was all wrong. Where was Callie, anyway? This was very wrong. Jenny knew she should swat him away. But she just . . . *couldn't*.

'Uh, do you know a lot about constellations?' she asked instead.

Easy moved his hand slightly, his thumb rubbing the base of her spine. *Wrong, wrong, wrong!* 'There's not much else to do in Lexington at night.' He sighed. 'Unless you want to climb up the water tower or throw shit onto the train tracks.'

'I'm from New York,' Jenny whispered, biting a tendril of her hair to keep her teeth from rattling with nervousness. 'Although you probably know that already.'

'Huh?'

'You know,' she shifted, her cheeks growing hot. It was horrifying to think that he'd already heard things – slutty things – about her.

'Nope. I don't. Are you famous?'

'I . . .' She cleared her throat. How could Yvonne know

the gossip about her and not this beautiful boy? 'No. I guess not.'

'Well, that's too bad.' Easy smiled. 'And here I thought I was in the presence of a celebrity.'

Jenny felt his hand on the small of her back again. It felt warm through the blanket.

'Jesus Christ!'

Jenny and Easy turned around quickly. *Mr Pardee*. The dorm mistress's husband, who also happened to be Waverly's most assholish French teacher, had pushed the door open all the way. Jenny saw a note scrawled on their white board: *Studying in Benny's room. Brett* Mr Pardee was dressed in a hooded Waverly football sweatshirt and a pair of red plaid pajama pants. His shaggy medium brown hair stood up in Brillo clumps on his head, and his tiny silver stud earring glinted in the harsh light of the hall.

Easy quickly jumped off Jenny's bed, pulled on his jeans, and grabbed his shirt.

'Dude.' He strode right up to Mr Pardee. 'I was never here.'

'You weren't . . . what?' Mr Pardee said, blinking furiously.

'You don't see me.'

'Easy, I *do* see you.' Pardee sounded as if he were trying to convince himself. 'You've used this line on me before.'

'Nope,' Easy replied. 'I was never here.' He dashed into the hall.

'Wait — where are you going?' Mr Pardee shouted. But it was too late. He shook his head and turned back to Jenny.

Not knowing exactly what to do, she hadn't moved. Mr Pardee might have been the dorm mistress's husband, but Jenny had heard he was also a total druggie. Supposedly, he only graded the French exams after smoking a spliff or two.

Maybe he was too wasted right now to even know what was going on?

'That wasn't cool.' Mr Pardee burped slightly. 'No guys in the room except during visiting hour.'

'I know, but—' Jenny sputtered.

'Man.' Mr Pardee was glaring at the condoms on the floor. No one had bothered to pick them up yet. 'This doesn't look good.'

'What's going on?' Callie stood in the doorway, right behind him.

'I'm gonna have to report this,' the teacher announced through a stoned yawn. 'I mean, Angelica will have to—'

'No, wait!' Jenny pleaded. She couldn't possibly be in trouble on the first day of school.

'Hello?' Callie repeated. 'What's going on?' Jenny noticed Mr Pardee eyeing the sliver of skin between Callie's low-hanging American Apparel shorts and her mesh Only Hearts camisole. The alligator on her bra peeked through its tiny holes.

'Easy was in here,' he stated matter-of-factly.

'Easy?!' Callie replied in a shocked tone, as if Mr Pardee had said, *I saw monkeys drinking beer*!

'Where were you?' Pardee asked.

Callie scowled and rolled her eyes. 'I was in the library. I'm just getting back.'

Jenny stared at her incredulously. Pardee seemed to buy this story, even though it was the middle of the night and Callie was hardly wearing any clothes, no shoes, and didn't have a backpack or any books on her.

'So what was Easy doing here?' Callie glared at Jenny as if to say, *Don't fuck this up.*

Mr Pardee raised an eyebrow. 'Well?'

A suspicious, hurt look clouded Callie's face. It was an acting job worthy of an Oscar. 'Was something . . . *going on?*'

Mr Pardee shuffled his feet. 'They were in bed together.'

'But we weren't *doing* anything!' Jenny defended.

'Then why does it look like a Costco-size box of condoms exploded in here?' Mr Pardee demanded.

Callie rolled her eyes. 'I can't believe it. You little bitch!' she shouted at Jenny, yanking up her shirt in frustration to expose her stomach. Mr Pardee stared hungrily at her field hockey-toned midriff. Callie wiggled her eyebrows at Jenny. *Keep going*, she mouthed.

Jenny's eyes widened. She wasn't going to let Callie make her take blame for this!

'Mr Pardee, this is a big misunderstanding,' Jenny pleaded, not even caring that the tone of her voice was getting squeaky. 'I really wasn't doing anything!'

But Mr Pardee shrugged. 'We'll find out in DC.'

'What?' Jenny said.

'Disciplinary Committee, *whore-bag*,' Callie spat.

'Callie, enough!' Mr Pardee commanded. 'Jenny, do you know who your adviser is?'

'It's, um, Mr Dalton?' That was what the welcome-to-Waverly letter addressed to Mister Jennifer Humphrey had said, anyway.

'Right. He's new. Okay. You'll report to Stansfield Hall to Mr Dalton's office at nine-thirty tomorrow. I'm not sure which room he's in, but check the map on the first floor. He'll evaluate your situation before it gets kicked up to DC.' He fiddled with his earring. 'Got that? Good. I have to go find Easy now . . .'

When she was sure he was gone, Callie shut the door and let out a huge sigh. 'Oh my God. So close.'

'*Whore-bag?*' Jenny's voice trembled.

'Sorry about that,' Callie sighed, sitting on her bed and staring at Jenny with her enormous hazel eyes. 'I had to make sure Mr Pardee believed I was pissed . . .'

'Well, he believed it all right.'

Callie shrugged. 'It's not a big deal.'

Jenny scrunched up her face. 'Not a big deal? I have to go in front of . . . a committee! What happens there, anyway?'

Callie leaned over and picked up one of the wrapped condoms. 'You're new, you're a girl, and I heard you're smart. They'll go easy on you.' She rubbed the square packet between her fingers. 'Maybe you could use your Raves connections.'

'What are you talking about?' Was Callie being sarcastic? Jenny had never even told Callie about the Raves. And what would the Disciplinary Committee make her do? Snorkel for trash in the Hudson? What if it went on her permanent record?

'Look,' Callie began. 'Brett's on the committee. She'll make sure you get off. If I'd gotten caught with Easy, they would've kicked me out. I've already been caught doing stuff here.'

'Oh?' Jenny said curiously.

'Yeah, I already have, like, two strikes against me. Three and you're out.'

'Oh.' Jenny felt somewhat relieved. So this was her first strike. That wasn't so bad.

'It would *really* suck if I got expelled.' Callie tore open the condom with her fingernail. 'My parents would make me to go public school in Atlanta. Kids sneak guns and cans of Miller Lite past the metal detectors there. And everyone's into NASCAR. Even the girls!' She stared down at Jenny. 'Could you imagine me at NASCAR?'

Callie was way too beautiful to go to public school. Then Jenny stopped herself, remembering she wasn't supposed to be all suck-uppy with an older girl the way Old Jenny had been with Serena van der Woodsen back at Constance. She closed her eyes and willed herself to stop. *New Jenny, New Jenny, New Jenny.*

Callie pulled out the yellowish condom and inserted her pointer finger into its open end. 'I have to make it through this year without getting busted.'

Jenny sighed resignedly. She loved everything about Waverly – the woodsiness, the New England-style brick buildings, that the teachers wore blazers to class and often had the title of doctor, even the succulent wasabi salmon that everybody shunned. She wanted to row on the river and go to the Spring Fling and meet boys from other prep schools and return to Manhattan triumphant, because she was now a boarding school girl. She didn't want it fucked up like this right off the bat, and yet here she was again, the most talked about girl on campus and already in trouble before classes had even started.

Callie twirled the condom around on her finger. 'Everything will be fine,' she assured Jenny. 'Seriously. They'll give you restricted study. Or no visitation. But Brett's on DC.' She smiled sweetly as if to say, *I'll be your best friend forever and ever if you help me out*.

'I just don't know.' Jenny wrung her hands in her lap. As much as she wanted to be friends with Callie, she didn't want to be in trouble. Not at all. 'I'll have to think about it.'

'I totally understand! Take your time! Think about it! But you aren't going to get in trouble. It's really, really, *really* not a big deal.'

'Yeah, but . . .' Jenny bit her lip. 'I don't know . . .'

Callie sprang off her bed, darted to her closet, and opened up the door. 'And here — for your meeting with your adviser tomorrow, you'll want to look as professional as possible. You want to borrow something of mine? Seriously. Anything.' She ran her hand down the rack of gorgeous, perfectly pressed designer clothes.

'Really?' Jenny stood up and peeked into Callie's closet with her. The weight of the situation slowly began to sink in. Would Callie have offered up anything in her closet before Mr Pardee had caught Easy in the room? No way.

Jenny felt a strange, heady rush of power, a rush so intense it kind of freaked her out.

'Seriously. Anything I can do. I'll totally make this the best year of your life,' Callie offered enthusiastically.

Jenny pulled a sleek black DKNY dress from off its white satin hanger and held it up to herself. The best year of her life? She could really use a year like that . . .

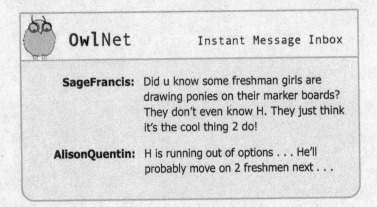

OwlNet   Instant Message Inbox

HeathFerro: So were they really having sex?? Could u hear them thru the walls?

EmilyJenkins: It was so LOUD I had to put my sound machine on city traffic to block out the noise!

HeathFerro: Were they knocking against the wall?

EmilyJenkins: Totally. I got negative sleep.

HeathFerro: Nice.

OwlNet   Instant Message Inbox

SageFrancis: Did u know some freshman girls are drawing ponies on their marker boards? They don't even know H. They just think it's the cool thing 2 do!

AlisonQuentin: H is running out of options . . . He'll probably move on 2 freshmen next . . .

12

A GOOD WAVERLY OWL LOOKS
HER SUPERIORS IN THE EYE.

The next morning, Jenny stood near the closets, surveying the quiet, sun-dappled dorm room. Today was only Thursday, the first day of classes, but already the room looked lived-in: books and papers everywhere, clothes heaped on the floor, makeup, shampoo and nail polish bottles strewn on top of desks next to flat-screen computer monitors, piles of notebooks and text-books, unopened packages of highlighters, and a large aloe plant teetering on the narrow windowsill. Jenny had arrived almost two days ago, but it still didn't feel like *her* dorm room, since she'd hardly had a moment in it alone. Brett's bed was empty — she'd snuck in after all the commotion last night and must have gotten up early.

There was an imprint in the mattress where her body had been. Callie was still sound asleep, curled up in the fetal position.

Jenny ran her hand over a pile of Callie's downy cashmere cardigans. All of Callie's clothes were beautiful, but this morning Jenny felt awkward about borrowing any of them. Instead, she slipped on her own Banana-Republic-but-looks-like-Theory shiny khaki circle skirt, her only Thomas Pink button-down shirt, and a pair of baby-pink Cynthia Rowley ballet flats. She put on her Waverly blazer and assessed the look. Definitely Not Guilty.

Jenny tiptoed into the hall and closed her dorm room door behind her. Next to Brett's note about studying in Benny's room, someone had written SAVE TINSLEY! in big magenta letters on the marker board hanging from the door. There was also a drawing of what looked like a little pony in the bottom corner. Walking down the hallway she noticed that some of the other girls' marker boards had little ponies drawn on them, too. Boarding school was turning out to be like a painting by Chagall – full of pranks, mind games, and mysteries.

Jenny wound her way along the ancient cobblestone paths that snaked through the Waverly campus toward Stansfield Hall, a massive brick structure that housed the administrative offices and a few classrooms. Few students were awake yet, but the maintenance crew was tending to the soccer field and the landscaping. The air smelled like freshly cut grass.

Inside Stansfield Hall there were intricate plaster moldings of creeping vines and flowers on the walls, stained-glass windows in the stairwells, and engravings in the wooden railings. Jenny climbed the stairs to the third floor and walked to the very end of a stately, mahogany-floored hall. A brass plate on the closed office door read ERIC DALTON. Inside, Jenny heard giggling and took a step back.

'I've heard that one before,' she heard a girl's voice say. 'Every English teacher since the sixth grade has told me that I share my name with the woman in *The Sun Also Rises*.'

'Lady Brett Ashley,' a man's voice said. 'She was a troublemaker.'

'Well, it must go with the name, then,' Jenny heard Brett answer in an extremely flirtatious voice.

'So, um, listen, we have to talk to this student, so we won't be able to get to some of the admin stuff I wanted to discuss. Are you free for lunch today? We could deal with it then.'

'I think so,' Brett replied. 'I'll meet you here?'

Jenny knocked on the door. She heard papers shuffling and the clink of glasses.

'Come in,' Mr Dalton called out. Jenny strode into the office, which was cramped and messy. Brett sat on the edge of a brown leather couch, her hands folded in her lap, looking way too prim and innocent.

Mr Dalton sat down at his desk chair and shuffled some papers. 'Jenny, right? Please, sit down.' He motioned to the couch. Jenny sat as far from Brett as she could. 'This is Brett,' he continued. 'She's on Disciplinary Committee and helping me with some administrative things.'

'Yeah, she's my—'

Brett turned to Mr Dalton. 'Jenny and I already know each other. We live in Dumbarton together.'

Yeah, in the same room. Jenny wondered why Brett didn't say they were roommates.

Dalton smiled. 'Oh, well, okay. Well, Brett is helping me out here with some DC issues, and as a member of DC, she's helping preside over this case.' He cleared his throat. 'So, Jenny, I'm your adviser, and I'm also gathering general facts about the DC case, so we're killing two birds with one stone here.' He flipped through some more papers as if he could somehow absorb what was written on them just by touching them.

Jenny noticed Brett wasn't wearing her Waverly jacket but a gorgeous, eggplant charmeuse silk top and a sleek, black knee-length wool skirt. On her feet were strappy Marc Jacobs sandals. Her long, thin legs were crossed sexily and angled toward Mr Dalton.

Mr Dalton perched on the corner of his desk with a legal pad in his hand. 'Okay, so what happened last night? We have you in your dorm room with a boy named Easy Walsh. Mr Pardee says you were lying in your bed together?'

'Well, that's the thing,' Jenny responded meekly. She'd stayed up all night weighing which was the better option: confirming the Waverly student body's suspicion that she was a giant slut or making enemies with her roommate. 'I don't . . . I don't think I'm ready to tell you what happened.'

Mr Dalton raised an eyebrow. 'Oh?'

'I mean, do I have to make a statement right now? Or

can it wait until, you know, the real hearing? Because I'm not really ready to talk about it.'

'Well, technically, you don't have to tell me anything,' Mr Dalton admitted, pen poised above the legal pad. 'Although, as your adviser, I'd like you to *feel* that you can tell me.'

'I'm not ready. I—'

'What do you mean you're not ready?' Brett interrupted, uncrossing her legs and glaring at Jenny. Her hair looked even redder when she was angry.

Jenny shut her mouth tight and shrugged her shoulders. She was afraid to speak.

Brett examined Jenny critically. Her pink and white striped button-down was too tight across her chest, and she was all pink-cheeked, as if she'd been running across a field.

Brett had come in late last night after the run-in with Mr Pardee, but Eric had filled her in when she arrived at his office this morning – not that Brett actually believed Pardee's version. It was totally stupid of Jenny not to say something to get her and Easy out of trouble. Poor Jenny. She was the perfect foil for Callie. God, Callie was a bitch.

Jenny noticed Brett inspecting her as if she were a biological specimen on a glass slide. She felt her cheeks grow hot. *I'm New Jenny, I'm New Jenny, I'm New Jenny*, she repeated silently, steeling herself.

'Well.' Mr Dalton rubbed his hands together. 'I guess if you don't want to say anything now, you certainly don't have to. But maybe there's someone else on the faculty you might feel more comfortable talking to?'

Jenny shrugged her shoulders again helplessly. Today was the first day of classes. She hadn't even met her teachers yet.

'Well then,' Mr Dalton continued, 'thanks for coming in, Jenny. I guess we'll have a full trial next week. How's Monday?'

'Yes, that's fine,' she replied hollowly. 'Um, thanks.' She glanced at Brett as she left Mr Dalton's office, hoping for an encouraging smile, but Brett was examining her fire-engine-red split ends, looking totally bored.

Jenny closed the heavy oak door behind her, wondering if it had been really stupid to tell them that she wasn't ready to make a statement. What was this, *Law & Order: Boarding School*?

All of a sudden, she was face-to-face with Easy Walsh, standing outside the door to Mr Dalton's office, waiting to come in. As soon as they locked eyes, her heart began to race.

She'd been so consumed with possibly getting in trouble and possibly being considered Waverly biggest slut ever that she'd let their intimate little back-rub session slide to the back of her mind. Now she remembered the nice warm feeling of Easy's body next to hers.

'Hey.' She swallowed quickly.

'Huh?' Easy stared at her blankly, his blue eyes droopy and tired-looking. He wore a tattered marigold-yellow T-shirt that read LEXINGTON ALL-STARS. 'Oh!' He widened his eyes.

'Um, how do you feel?' Jenny persisted shyly.

'I . . .' He lurched off to the left, his eyes still wide. A strong smell of stale vodka was oozing out his pores. 'I . . . you were just in there?'

'Yes.' Jenny felt tipsy just breathing the same air as Easy.

He started to say something else, but then the door opened, and Mr Dalton stuck his blond head out. 'Mr Walsh, it's your turn.'

Without saying goodbye, Easy staggered into the office. Jenny turned and padded down the stairs into the bright sunshine. On a low tree branch directly above the pathway sat one of those fat great horned owls. She froze. Was this the same one that had tried to kill her just two days ago? She narrowed her eyes.

The owl finally blinked slowly at her, as if it were stoned, then looked away.

Jenny hurried past it on her way to her first class. It was the first and possibly only triumphant moment of the day. She'd won a staring contest with an owl.

13

IN TIMES OF EMOTIONAL DISTRESS, A WAVERLY OWL SHOULD LISTEN TO HIS INNER OWL.

'Glad to see you could make it,' Dalton greeted Easy. Last night's Ketel One binge had left Easy feeling like the gunk he picked out of Credo's feet before a ride. He slumped into a black leather Eames office chair and stared blankly at Callie's roommate, Brett, who was seated across from him in a totally see-through purple blouse. His new adviser looked about eighteen, a welcome change from his old adviser, Mr Kelley, who was so ancient he could barely remember his own name and had finally retired last year at the age of about a hundred.

'Hello, Easy,' Brett greeted him in an exaggerated authoritative tone, making a few notes in a yellow steno pad. 'Have a good summer?'

'Uh-huh,' Easy grunted, staring up at the ceiling. Brett might have thought she was Miss I-have-power-over-you-because-I'm-a-prefect, but Easy wasn't buying it. He and Brett used to be close. They'd had French class together freshman year, and for the final discussion presentation, instead of getting up in front of the class and having an inane conversation, Brett had had the idea to make a morbid, Godardian French-phrase short film with an antique Super-8 camera. Easy was her partner for the class and therefore the existential star of the film. He got to say weird stuff in French like, '*Mon omelette du jambon est mort*', and, '*Les yeux* – the eyes – are in pain.' Monsieur Grimm had loved it and had given them both A's.

'E. Francis Walsh,' Dalton addressed him, eyeing his file carefully. 'What do you want to tell me about last night?'

'With her here?' He pointed a thumb at Brett. 'I thought these things were confidential.'

'I'm his assistant,' Brett jumped in quickly, sitting up straighter.

'She's helping me with Disciplinary Committee procedures,' Dalton explained. 'I think this qualifies.'

Easy looked back and forth between them. Whoa. Dalton was whipped – by Brett Messerschmidt!

'It says here that you've had quite a few problems with the rules over the last few years, Easy.' Dalton cleared his throat. 'Disciplinary probation three times. Suspension twice.

You were nearly kicked out once last year for not showing up to class after spring break. Countless arguments with teachers. Bad attitude.' He paused and flipped to a new page of the file. 'Disruptive in class. Subpar grades. Almost no extracurricular activities. Caught with alcohol four times. Skipping sports practice. No team spirit . . .' He turned to another page.

Brett smirked.

'But . . .' Mr Dalton held his index finger to the file and raised his eyebrows. He showed the paper to Brett and she cocked her head skeptically. Easy rolled his eyes. No doubt it was those fucking PSAT scores again. So he'd scored nearly perfect in all three sections – big deal. It was the kind of thing his parents salivated over, even though Easy couldn't have cared less. Sneaking out of the dorm to watch shooting stars in the middle of the practice fields at two in the morning or walking barefoot in the creek behind the arts building at dawn – those were the kinds of things he cared about, things that he could remember when he was old and shaky. Not some stupid test score. Unfortunately, all the bullshit rules got in the way, when all Easy wanted was more perfect Waverly moments like those.

'You're a legacy,' Dalton went on, glancing at his knotted cuff links. 'But that shouldn't mean anything. I mean, I'm a Waverly legacy too.'

'Really?' Brett squealed. 'So am I!'

'My dad went here and my grandfather went here. And his brother too.' Dalton turned to Brett. 'Basically, the Dalton men were Waverly Academy's first graduating class.'

'As if I needed to know,' Easy muttered sarcastically. What was up with this teacher trying to impress Brett?

Dalton narrowed his eyes. 'Look, I never expected to be treated any differently than anybody else. In fact, I think the teachers were harder on me because I was a legacy — they expected me to be an example for the other students.'

'Right.' Wasn't *that* a load of bullshit. Easy gritted his teeth. He was a legacy, which was supposed to be this special thing, but he knew how it really worked: if your family had enough money to send successive kids (or generations) to Waverly, the administration would kiss your ass for the rest of your days. There weren't any moral standards involved, just money. Heath Ferro was a goddamn legacy, after all, and look at all the shit he'd pulled!

Dalton leaned forward. 'Scoff all you want, but you shouldn't have been in Dumbarton last night, and you certainly shouldn't have been . . . er . . . with that new girl Jennifer Humphrey.'

'Were you with Jenny?' Brett leaned forward, looking extremely interested.

'What did Jenny say about that?' Easy asked.

'She didn't say anything.' Brett frowned. 'She said she wasn't ready to make a statement.'

'Oh.' Easy scratched his nose. He wasn't sure what to make of Jenny and what had happened last night. After talking to her in the cafeteria, he'd convinced himself she was just a mirage. She didn't look like she wore much makeup, if any, and she was tiny, where Callie was tall. She had miniature hands and feet, long eyelashes, and she carried around a bag that didn't have big Gucci G's plastered all over it. And she'd asked him about art. Callie wouldn't dream of asking him about art. And last night – well that had been a mirage too – a drunken one. He'd been about to score with Callie and had wound up scurrying half-naked out of Jenny's bed, with Pardee on his tail.

Now Jenny – pretty little Jenny – was in trouble because of him. But he'd needed to be near her. She looked so pink and new, sort of like that Botticelli painting he'd seen in Rome last year: *The Birth of Venus*, with the sexy chick coming out of the clamshell. He didn't want her to be in trouble. But he didn't want Callie to find out he'd touched Jenny, either. Easy gripped his head in his hands to keep his hungover brains from spilling out of his ears.

'So listen, I don't know what's going on here, but as your adviser, I have to warn you: this sort of offense, on top of your myriad other offenses, could lead to expulsion.'

Brett sucked in her breath and shook her head, pretending to actually care.

Easy barely blinked. 'Okay.'

'Did you hear what I just said?' Dalton asked. 'You might be expelled.'

'Yeah. I heard you.'

'If I were you, I'd spend more time thinking about why I was here,' Dalton suggested sternly, 'and less time getting in trouble.'

That was the kind of dick thing one of his brothers might say. Easy was the youngest of four, and his three brothers had all gone to Waverly as well. Whenever Easy complained to them about it, they'd say that he wouldn't understand the importance of Waverly until he got out. Which was one of those bullshit things people said when they got older and brainwashed. His brothers had already graduated from college and law school; two were married and the other one was engaged. They were pussy-whipped, boring adults and didn't know a thing about *really* living.

'Fine,' Easy replied through his teeth. 'You done advising me, then?' Without waiting for an answer, he stood up forcefully, yanked the door open, and strode out.

Outside Stansfield Hall, he felt suddenly light-headed. *You might be expelled.* Was he serious? If Easy got kicked out of Waverly, he could forget about his year in Paris. He'd be forced to live at home, alone with his crusty parents, where he'd be schooled by a private tutor and his only contact with the outside world would be the scary frosted-blond mail lady who liked Easy a little *too* much. Easy needed to sit down. Maybe it was the vodka from last night, but he felt a whoosh of nausea.

Hoot, hoot.

Easy looked up into the trees. One of the great horned owls was watching him, its eyes round and yellow. Easy made a cooing sound at it, like the one he made when he needed Credo to calm down, and pulled a dented Sprite bottle out of his school bag. He took a swig of the remaining Ketel One from last night. Everyone was making their way to the first classes of the year, but Easy needed to think.

He wandered along the worn stone path toward the stables, wishing Callie would be there to lie down with him in a humid corral and make him forget all about Dalton's threat. They'd stretch out on an old horse blanket and stay there all day, not caring about missing the first day of classes. But picturing Callie naked in the abandoned stable wasn't getting him excited – he couldn't stop Fantasy Callie from complaining about hay in her hair and imaginary bugs on the blanket.

Easy closed himself into the warm, slightly moist corral, and squeezed his eyes shut. But when he revisited his fantasy, it wasn't Callie sprawled across the horse blanket, staring up at him.

It was Jenny.

OwlNet

To: Waverly Students
From: DeanMarymount@waverly.edu
Date: Thursday, September 5, 9:01 A.M.
Subject: Property defacement

Dear Students,

It has come to my attention that pony drawings have shown up around campus – on the sidewalks, on marker boards, and on the shower walls of the girls' locker room.

Please know that defacement of Waverly property is a serious offense and will not be tolerated. A few students have anonymously reported emotional distress over them, as well. Please be advised that the mental health center is open twenty-four hours a day and that anyone seen defacing school property will face disciplinary consequences.

Enjoy your first day of classes,

Dean Marymount

14

NO WAVERLY OWL ESCAPES QUESTIONING —
EVEN IF SHE IS A GOVERNOR'S DAUGHTER.

Callie was spacing out through first-period Latin
when Mrs Tullington, the school's administrator,
interrupted class. 'Ms Vernon,' Mr Gaston, the
teacher, addressed her. 'Your adviser wants to see you.'

Her adviser's office was only one floor down from the
Latin room. Callie nervously rubbed her palms together.
She and Ms Emory weren't exactly buddy-buddy. Ms Emory
was a short-haired, middle-aged, dykey bitch from
Connecticut who had gone to Vassar with Callie's mother.
The two women had been rivals, always vying for the
highest GPA and admission into Phi Beta Kappa. They'd
also fought for the same spot at Harvard Law — and Callie's
mom had won. Bitter, Ms Emory had decided to forgo law

school and instead had gotten her master's in education at NYU. She'd made it very clear to Callie that missing out on Harvard had affected the entire course of her life, and Callie suspected she blamed this all on her mother. It was another brilliant student-adviser match by the Waverly administration.

Ms Emory's office was freaky. She had absolutely no books or personal affects on her shelves, and the only thing tacked to her bulletin board was the Waverly call sheet, which listed all of the other faculty members' office numbers and extensions. A lonely flat-screen Sony Vaio rested on her dark wooden desk, and a shopping bag with the words RHINECLIFF YARN BARN across the front sat on a bare table behind her. Wooden knitting needles and some tan yarn peeked out from the top. Ms Emory, a knitter? How random.

Callie sat down quickly on the black Aeron chair opposite Ms Emory's desk. Next to her adviser's Spartan-looking all-black turtleneck and practical black pants, Callie's sheer pink flouncy Diane von Furstenberg skirt and pink-diamond-encrusted Chopard watch seemed ridiculous.

'You wanted to see me?'

Ms Emory looked up from her computer keyboard. She squinted one eye and contorted her gigantic mouth into a sneer. She looked like a deranged female Popeye. Why couldn't Callie have gotten a nice adviser, like Mrs Swan, who took her advisees to the Metropolitan Opera three times a year, or Mr Bungey, who threw his kids Scotch-tasting Christmas parties and listened to all their relationship problems? Oh no, she had to get the crazy Popeye lady, who probably used those knitting needles to poke her advisees in the ass when they misbehaved.

'Mr Pardee told me I should talk to you,' Ms Emory announced flatly. 'He said that your boyfriend was caught in your room last night. After curfew.'

Callie took a deep breath to prepare herself. She'd had years of practice bending the truth for her mother, but it always made her nervous. 'Well, that's the thing,' she began. 'My boyfriend was there, yes. But he wasn't visiting me. He was visiting my roommate, Jenny.'

'And how do you know that?'

Callie furrowed her brow. 'Because . . . because I wasn't there.'

Ms Emory gave her a look of disbelief. '*Umhmm.*' She began to type something on her keyboard. Callie noticed she had very stubby nails, chewed way down to the quick.

Shit. Did Ms Emory's *umhmm* mean Jenny had told on her? Callie didn't think so: she'd seen the gleam in her eye – Jenny was hungry. Why else would she have shown up at the Richards dorm party, basically uninvited? If she didn't care about the Waverly social order, she'd go and be friends with that dorky Yvonne girl. No, Jenny wanted more than that, Callie was certain.

'Look.' Callie shrugged. 'I don't know what went on. I was studying. It was right before curfew, and I came back and only Jenny was there. Easy had left. Mr Pardee was talking to her.'

'Mmmm. So, then. You and Easy, you're not a couple anymore?'

Callie winced. With that horrible *I love you* still hanging out there, unanswered, every second that went by without him saying it back made her feel ridiculously vulnerable. If they didn't have sex soon and start talking about how much they loved each other, Callie might have to check herself into the mental health center along with all the girls traumatized by the ponies on their boards.

'No,' Callie lied. 'We're not together.'

'Really.' Ms Emory stared at her over her square black glasses. 'Because someone spotted you and Mr Walsh at the stables only yesterday.'

'We . . . we were breaking up,' Callie managed to stutter, her voice dry. 'I . . . I don't really want to talk about it, if that's okay.' *Damn that Ben!* Damn the faculty and staff for living with the students on campus and knowing every freaking intimate detail of their lives!

'Mm,' Ms Emory replied, looking as if she didn't believe Callie at all. 'Well, behave. We haven't forgotten about last year.'

'Okay,' Callie squeaked.

Then Ms Emory began to type furiously. Generally this was Callie's cue to leave. She badly wanted to crane her neck around to see what she was typing – probably a three-point plan for how to ruin Callie's life.

She raced back to class, eager to be back in the soothing world of Latin verb declensions. Seated at her desk, she rubbed her hands together. If Ms Emory found out she'd lied and that Easy had been there to see her, she'd definitely be expelled, especially after last year's E episode. Then her mother would disown her and she'd have to go live with her fishy-smelling Aunt Brenda in the most boring suburb of Atlanta. She'd be forced to go to Catholic school with pale, zitty kids who thought a big night out was drinking Smirnoff Ice in the Dairy Queen parking lot and trading NASCAR cards. Callie's stomach turned.

She had two challenges before her: one, making sure Jenny didn't talk, and two, convincing Ms Emory that she and Easy weren't an item. Her life at Waverly depended on it.

OwlNet

To: JennyHumphrey@waverly.edu
From: KissKiss! Online
Date: Thursday, September 5, 12:50 P.M.
Subject: Surprise!

Dear Jenny Humphrey,

It's your lucky day! Your friend Callie Vernon has selected a beauty gift basket for you, full of $50 worth of makeup. The basket comes with a free Le Sportsac tote! Please go to our Web site to pick the color you'd like.

Kiss kiss,

The KissKiss! staff

OwlNet   Instant Message Inbox

CallieVernon: Come with me to Pimpernels. Noon.

EasyWalsh: Shopping? No.

CallieVernon: It's important. We need to talk.

EasyWalsh: Can't we talk on campus?

CallieVernon: U can come into the dressing room with me . . .

EasyWalsh: Aren't we in enough shit already?

15

A WAVERLY OWL SHOULD ALWAYS
TAKE THE MORAL HIGH ROAD.

Easy saw Callie leaning up against the storefront, nervously fiddling with her bamboo-handled Gucci bag and holding an unlit cigarette. It was a warm afternoon, and she was wearing a colorful flimsy shirt and matching skirt. Rhinecliff locals – mostly scraggly-haired hippie artists – were milling about the cobblestone street, eating strawberry ice cream cones from the creamery and stopping to talk to Hank, the guy who sold tie-dyed T-shirts and incense on the sidewalk. Easy doubted the hippies were talking to Hank for the incense, though. Hank sold pot to plenty of Waverly students, including Easy. He'd already waved his hello.

'Well, look who's here,' Callie said sarcastically.

Easy didn't answer. They were in front of Pimpernel's, a frou-frou boutique Callie deigned to shop at. It was the only store in Rhinecliff that didn't usually sell tie-dyed shirts – and when it did, they were silk, sequined, and cost $300. The last time he'd been here, Easy had spent the whole time examining a tiny pink knitted socklike thing that cost $360, trying to figure out what it could possibly be. A nose warmer? A bag for pot? A snuggly condom? Callie had finally informed him that it was a cashmere dog bootie.

It was important that he talk to Callie, though, so here he was. 'We're in trouble,' he announced flatly.

Callie examined her freshly manicured nails. '*We*, huh?'

Easy scowled. 'Of course *we*. And why did I see Jenny Humphrey come out of Dalton's office? Was it for last night? She had nothing to do with this.'

'Well, Ms Emory called me in too. And if you must know, yes, Jenny was in there because of last night. It's not like I can take the rap. The E thing, remember? My parents would disown me and send me to NASCAR school!'

'What are you talking about?' Easy demanded, rubbing the unshaven sides of his face.

Callie shook her mane of blond hair off the back of her neck. 'Look, I don't want to get kicked out. So I said you were there with Jenny and that we had broken up.'

'*What?*' Easy asked, stunned. Callie shrugged and pushed open the door to the store. Chimes jingled to announce their arrival.

'Sweetheart! Welcome back!' shrieked a very tall, very thin woman with slicked-back blond hair as soon as they stepped through the door.

'Hi, Tracey!' Callie cooed. They kissed each other's cheeks in a well-rehearsed routine. Easy hung back, wanting out. Immediately. Shopping, screaming girls, cashmere dog booties — so not his thing. Why had he come? He should be enjoying his last days at Waverly.

'I held some things for you over the summer.' Tracey beckoned, whisking Callie and Easy into a little back alcove. She brought out a garment rack of shiny dresses, skirts, and blouses. She held up an ivory Donna Karan gown. 'Isn't this pretty?'

Easy turned his head to the side to read the price tag: $2,250.

'Oh, yes,' Callie breathed. She didn't seem at all concerned that she'd gotten her new roommate in trouble or that she'd lied to the administration. Nope. All she was worried about was whether this dress came in a small enough size.

'You could practically wear this to your wedding!' Tracey shoved the dress up against Callie's body.

'If you were a hooker,' Easy added rudely. He plopped down onto the lavender couch, pulling a frilly, pink-lace pillow out from under his ass.

Callie rolled her eyes. 'Boys,' she sighed at Tracey. 'They know nothing!' Then she walked over and stroked Easy's arm. 'So, was Dalton mean to you?'

'He said I might get kicked out.'

'Oh, but you won't. You're a legacy. They never kick out legacies.' Easy saw a flicker of worry cross her face as she gathered up the dresses Tracey had given her to try on.

'I don't know,' he responded as she closed the pink dressing room door. 'What if they decide to set a new precedent?'

'They won't,' Callie insisted determinedly, throwing her nude La Perla bra over the top of the dressing room door. It looked flimsy and a little sad. 'You're definitely safe.'

'So you're just going to let Jenny take the rap for you then?'

'Why not? Mr Pardee caught her, after all. And she's prepared. We discussed it.'

Easy sighed. 'You know, Dalton told me she didn't say one way or another what happened. So what if she tells?'

'She won't,' Callie called back, her voice cracking with forced determination.

Easy sat back. The shopkeeper, Tracey, stared at his Converse high-tops, which he'd propped up on the store's lavender velvet ottoman. What, was he not supposed to put his feet there? Tough.

Suddenly, Callie stuck her head out of the dressing room door. 'Sweetie? I need you to do me a teeny, tiny little favor.'

'What?' If it was to help her untangle her thong or zip something up, he really wasn't in the mood.

Callie's eyes met his. 'Well . . .' She curled a strand of blond hair around her forefinger. 'If Jenny's going to take the rap for me – and I'm sure she will – we need things to look . . . believable.'

'Believable?'

'You know. Like something *actually* happened between you two.'

Easy rolled his jaw around incredulously, staring at her.

'So,' Callie breezed ahead, 'this might sound weird, but I'm wondering if you might flirt with her a little. You know, maybe if you two acted like you liked each other. Just a little.'

'You're asking me to flirt with another girl?' Easy laughed, taking his feet off the velvet ottoman. 'Have you forgotten you're the most jealous person on the planet?'

Callie closed the door again and slung the dress she'd just been wearing over the top. 'I am not jealous,' she retorted.

'What do you want me to do?'

'I don't know. Flirt. Be nice to her. Friendly.'

With the dressing-room door closed, Callie's view of Easy was obscured. But if she could have seen him, she might have been confused by the seemingly huge, googly grin on his face and the rising color spreading up his neck to his cheeks.

When she stuck her head out of the door again, he'd managed to compose himself.

'Does that really sound so bad? You're not going to get kicked out of school. That's just silly. But you were already seen by Mr Pardee in the dorm, so you're *already* in trouble. It wouldn't hurt to make it a teensy bit believable, would it?'

'Well, they're right!' Easy put his hands in the air help-lessly.

She jiggled up and down out of frustration, and Easy looked at her chest for a second. 'Sweetie, please? Wouldn't that be awful if I got kicked out?'

'But what if *I* get kicked out?'

Callie screwed up her face. 'You won't,' she said firmly. 'I already told you that.'

Easy hesitated. Was it possible that Callie had somehow seen him sitting on Jenny's bed last night, touching her back, and that this was all a test? Better to play it like he wasn't sure about the idea – although inside, of course, his whole body felt like it had been struck by lightning. Was it really possible that his girlfriend was actually asking him to get to know the girl he was digging? 'This doesn't sound very moral,' he answered stoically, keeping the shit-eating smile off his face.

'Moral?' She slammed the door shut again. 'Are we forgetting about how you stole me away from Brandon Buchanan last year? Right out from under his nose?'

'So?'

'That wasn't exactly moral, was it?'

Easy shrugged.

'Anyway,' Callie continued, 'I'm going to tell Jenny about it, too. It's not like I'm asking you to make out with her or anything. Will you *please* just do this for me?'

'I . . .' Easy croaked. She wasn't testing him. She was serious. He really was the fucking luckiest guy in the world.

Callie opened the door, wearing the white Donna Karan

dress. She looked like Boarding-School-Bitch Barbie on her wedding day. 'So you'll do it?' she asked. He slowly nodded, and she broke into a smile. 'Thank you, sweetie. It'll be a humungous help.'

No, no, Easy thought. Thank you.

OwlNet   Email Inbox

To: RufusHumphrey@poetsonline.com
From: JennyHumphrey@waverly.edu
Date: Thursday, September 5, 12:15 P.M.
Subject: Miss you

Hi Dad,

I just had my first English class. My teacher read part of 'Howl' aloud and it made me think of when we snuck your gross-looking but yummy oatmeal cookies into that weird movie place and watched that documentary on Allen Ginsberg. I loved that day.

Field hockey tryouts were yesterday and you're not going to believe this but I'm a total natural. Did you secretly coach a hockey for beat poets team or something? Because I don't know where I get it from . . .

I'm still adjusting to everything here – it's different from the city and Constance in so many ways. Smells much better and there are no roaches, but there are lots of RULES – I'm still learning what they are . . . Let's hope I pick up on them as quickly as field hockey.

Have you heard from Dan?? I admit I even miss him sometimes.

Hugs and kisses!

Love you,

Jenny

P.S. Can you send my cell phone? I thought they weren't allowed, but as it turns out, everyone has them here. It's on top of my bureau in my room. And if it happened to magically turn into a Treo 650, well, I wouldn't send it back . . . Thanks, Dad. Love you again.

16

A CLEVER WAVERLY OWL
CAN HANDLE ANYTHING.

'So tell me about this hot teacher,' Brett's sister cooed. Brett had ducked behind Stansfield Hall to make a quick cell phone call to the *Elle* offices before rejoining Eric for lunch. 'You're going to have *lunch* with him?'

'It's a *working* lunch,' Brett said. 'We ran out of time this morning. It doesn't *mean* anything.'

'Sure it does! What's his name, anyway?'

'Eric Dalton?'

'What? You cut out for a sec.'

'Eric Dalton,' Brett continued loudly again, and then took the phone away from her ear to look at the screen. The screen flashed CALL LOST. She shoved her Nokia back into her bag.

Brett couldn't help but feel nervous. She hadn't been able to stop thinking about Eric since they'd met yesterday. He was a little awkward and aloof, which was a challenge. Brett also had a sense that he liked her but that he knew that he shouldn't – another challenge. Brett liked challenges.

This morning, in calc, as Mr Farnsworth was explaining the concept of infinity, Brett had imagined them sneaking away to New York City, snagging the presidential suite at the Sherry-Netherland, ordering Veuve Clicquot champagne and eggs Benedict from room service, and having hours and hours of sweaty sex with the curtains wide open so they could watch the horse-drawn carriages in the park.

The one time she and Jeremiah had gone out in the city, Brett had wanted to get a Martini at Harry Cipriani, which was right in the Sherry-Netherland Hotel. But Jeremiah had demanded they go to Smith & Wollensky because he knew the Yankees-Sox game would be blaring from their plasma-screen TV. Her stomach flopped when she thought about Jeremiah coming over this afternoon. She wasn't in the right frame of mind to see him.

Brett gritted her teeth as she climbed up the stairs toward Eric's office. All she wanted to do was sit on Callie's bed, drink her signature banana daiquiri protein shake straight from the blender, and tell her about every freckle on Eric's perfect face. But since they'd moved in, she and Callie had hardly spoken. She'd tried to ask Callie about the Jenny/Easy thing when she'd stopped by the dorm after the morning meetings, but Callie had quickly rushed to the showers without answering. So what, they weren't friends now? Or maybe Callie was afraid that if she let her guard down, she'd confess what she'd done to Tinsley? Probably.

Brett knocked on Eric's office door and smelled chamomile tea brewing inside. He flung the door open and broke into an adorable grin.

'Hey,' he said, stepping back to let her pass.

Brett smiled back at him, willing herself not to throw her arms around his tan, sexy neck. He looked gorgeous, from his neatly knotted tie to his . . . argyle socks. No shoes, just green, soft-looking argyle socks. Her insides quivered. Because after all, right underneath that layer of what she bet was Brooks Brothers cashmere, were his feet. He was basically one step away from being naked.

'Thanks,' she replied, regaining her composure. Then she noticed an enormous tray of cheese, caviar, olives, smoked salmon, crackers and tea cakes teetering on the edge of the credenza. It was exactly the kind of opulent array of gourmet goodies her father's clients sent to her parents' house in a basket as thanks for their lipo tune-ups.

'You like cheese? Manchego? Coach Triple Cream?'

As if she could actually eat. 'Sure. All of it.'

'Olives, too?' He pointed. 'I like having little picnics.'

Brett demurely took a tiny sliver of cheese and popped it between her plump lips. The salt coated her mouth and she swallowed noisily.

'I got into eating this way from my family.' Eric scratched

the side of his slender, clean-shaven neck. 'My family, man. They're crazy about cheese.'

'Yeah,' Brett agreed, mesmerized by his classic New England accent. She didn't have any idea where he was from, but it had to be somewhere on the East Coast. Boston, maybe, but he most definitely did not speak with a townie accent. 'What do your parents do?' She finally managed to say.

He paused. 'Uh, well, my dad works in magazine publishing. My mom . . . she has her little projects, I guess. Yours?'

Talk about vague. 'My dad's a doctor.' Brett shrugged. She wasn't about to tell Dalton a doctor of what. 'And my mom . . . yeah. She has her little projects too.' One of those projects being buying designer sweaters for the seven family Chihuahuas.

'So, my sources say you've been to Italy,' Eric said, spreading Brie onto a Breton wafer and sitting back down in his chair.

Brett looked up at him. 'Yeah. How'd you know that?'

He ducked his head a little shyly. 'Well, I mean, I saw it in your file.'

She felt color rising to her cheeks. Duh. Of course he'd looked at her file. That was how he'd recognized her in first place. Did that mean he knew about her parents?

'I'm sorry,' he added quickly. 'I didn't mean to—'

'No!' she said. 'God. I don't care. I went to Europe through school. I spent some time in South America, too, with family.' She didn't add that her family had bought the biggest, tackiest house in Buzios, Brazil, and flown all the Chihuahuas first class to spend the summer with them.

He looked at her seriously. 'You're modest. You went to France with the advanced French students – mostly seniors – when you were a sophomore – and you went to Crete with the honors program when you were a freshman.'

She shrugged. It was weird having someone repeat your achievements back to you. But kind of cool, too. Jeremiah probably had no idea where Crete even was.

'You're smart.' He smiled. 'I need a smart woman around helping me get through this first year.'

'Well, that's me,' she said sheepishly, feeling a little funny that he'd called her a woman instead of a girl. She watched as he gracefully deposited an olive pit on the edge of the Italian-looking blue ceramic tray. Jeremiah would've spit it out in his hand.

'So, let's get started.' He flipped his manila folder open and revealed a big stack of papers. 'I want to show you this – these are some of the case files. They're like nine thousand pages long. And seriously, keep this quiet. Remember, you're not technically supposed to be doing this kind of work, since you weren't on DC last year. Everything in these files is confidential. Think you can handle that?'

'Absolutely,' Brett assured him. She laughed lightly. 'I'm good with secrets.'

'Yeah?' He looked up at her and broke into a slow smile. Brett felt her insides melt. He handed her a pile of papers, his fingers brushing the back of her hand. Brett nearly choked on her Manchego. He didn't pull away very fast, either. Time slowed down. Brett counted: *One Mississippi, two Mississippi* . . .

Three seconds. Their hands were still touching. Tingles ran the whole way up her back and her hand hummed as if she were touching an electric fence.

'I was hoping you might be,' he murmured, finally breaking the silence.

Brett looked down, willing her lips not to break into an enormous grin.

WAVERLY OWLS SHOULD BE CAREFUL
WHOM THEY TELL THEIR SECRETS TO.

Brandon spied Jenny in the distance, coming over the dewy green hill from Hunter Hall, the English building. She'd carefully arranged her long curly hair into two perky braids and was wearing a pink and white button-down shirt, her Waverly jacket, and a cute little khaki skirt. Brandon could almost imagine her as a farm girl, on her way to milk a cow or sing on a hilltop.

Two blond ponytailed girls hugged their books to their chests and smiled at him as they passed. 'Hey, Brandon,' Sage Francis, an ice blonde in an ultrashort dove-gray pleated skirt and silver sandals, cooed. Brandon smiled distractedly. 'Saw you eating dinner last night with that Jenny girl. Did she really sleep with the guy from the White Stripes?'

'What?' Brandon asked, scratching an artfully tweezed eyebrow.

'I heard she slept with the lead singer from the Raves, Jack White, and Easy Walsh – all in one week!'

'And don't forget, she was ponied!' shrieked Sage's friend, a girl named Helena who was well known for starring in school plays and making out with the student director at the cast parties. Brandon was a little tired of the term *pony*. All the girls were throwing it around and acting completely ridiculous about it. Worse, Heath *loved* that they'd made up a sex term just for him. Last night, before heading to dinner, Heath had poked Brandon in his power yoga-toned abs and boasted, 'You wanna bet I can pony someone between first and second courses?'

'She didn't say anything happened between her and Easy,' Brandon replied evenly, trying to sound calm.

'She's worse than Tinsley!' Sage and Helena giggled, then linked hands and walked off.

'No she——' Brandon started. But they were already gone. Personally, Brandon felt nauseated over all the rumors about Jenny. He'd heard she'd been caught having loud sex with Easy Walsh last night wearing nothing but a lacy push-up bra on the roof of her dorm – the rumors were all over Waverly. Not that he believed Jenny had done it – she was way too sweet to do something like that. Especially with a dog like Easy Walsh.

Jenny was still walking toward him, looking even more innocent and wide-eyed than when Brandon had first met her. He reached out and caught her arm as she passed. 'Hey.'

Jenny stopped, deep in a daze. 'Oh!' she exclaimed. Now that she was looking at him, he could see the dark purple circles under her eyes. He wished he could gently pat his L'Occitane Open Eyes Magic Eye Balm onto her delicate skin. 'Hey.'

'You okay?'

'Um, sure.'

'I got you this.' He searched through his John Varvatos tan suede satchel and found a turkey-and-Brie sandwich wrapped in a dining hall napkin. 'I didn't see you at lunch, and I thought you might be hungry.'

'Yeah, I was e-mailing my dad.' Jenny pressed her lips together, not looking him in the eye. 'It's just . . . I'm kind of ready to crack under the pressure,' she admitted, her lips trembling. 'I don't know what to do.'

'What happened?'

'Never mind.' Jenny shook her head, her chin quivering. 'I'm all right. I just have to think about things for a while, you know?'

Brandon wondered what she meant. Did this mean she had been with Easy after all? Or that someone was just spreading vicious unfounded rumors about her? Easy, probably. God, he hated Easy.

'Don't let him get to you,' Brandon said, trying to look into Jenny's big brown eyes.

'Who?'

'You know. Easy.'

'Easy? This really isn't Easy's fault.' Jenny kicked at the perfectly manicured green.

'No? Then is it the pony stuff? Because you know, practically every girl at Waverly has made the mistake of hooking up with Heath.' Brandon smiled a little. 'Seriously. They'll find someone else to talk about soon.'

Jenny shook her head and looked up at him through her think black eyelashes. 'I didn't even know he was called Pony,' she confessed dejectedly. 'But at least I know what those drawings mean now. Anyway, no, it's not only Heath. That was just the start of it.'

'Then what is it?'

'I feel like . . .' Jenny swallowed hard. She was sort of embarrassed to admit this to someone she hardly knew, but she felt like she could trust Brandon. 'I feel like Easy and I could have a real connection. It's weird. I can't explain it.'

Brandon felt his throat close up. *What. The. Fuck.* 'So,' he finally got out. 'You . . . like him?'

'Well, I . . .' Her voice trailed off.

Brandon shook his head vigorously. 'You can't like Easy.'

Jenny shrugged. 'Well, yeah. I know. He's my roommate's boyfriend.'

Yes, he was well aware of that, thank you very much. *But no, you shouldn't like him because he's fucking bad news.* After all, Easy had stolen Callie from him last year and nothing had been the same since. One minute, she was standing next to him at the party at the library, asking for a Grey Goose and tonic. The next, she was ascending the library stairs, with Easy's tongue practically down her throat in public.

Now Jenny had some sort of connection with him? Puh-lease.

'It doesn't matter, anyway.' She stared down at her shoes and squeezed her eyes shut. 'I shouldn't have said anything.'

'No . . .' Brandon offered lamely. 'I'm glad you did.'

'I have to go,' she said, still pouting at the ground. 'I hope your day goes okay.' Her voice quivered again, as if she were about to cry.

For maybe the second time in his life, Brandon wanted to punch a hole in something. Why did Easy steal every cool girl? And did this mean something *had* happened between them?

Brandon's next class was molecular and cell biology, and he was two minutes late. He slid into his seat and glared viciously at the girl with long blond hair sitting in front of him. She wore a sparkly amethyst ring on her right hand and smelled vaguely of cigarettes and Jean Patou Joy perfume. She turned and twisted the corners of her pretty, pouty, Chanel-glossed mouth up into a half-smile.

'Hey, Brandon,' Callie chirped. 'Meet any nice girls this summer?'

Brandon shrugged, averting his eyes to watch a flock of geese flap by the classroom's picture window on their way south, honking their heads off. He hadn't met any nice girls over the summer, but he'd met one on his first day back at school. How could he prevent Waverly from ruining Jenny the way it had ruined Callie?

OwlNet Instant Message Inbox

BennyCunningham:	So they're not even speaking to each other anymore.
CelineColista:	Did you see the SAVE TINSLEY! on their board?
BennyCunningham:	I think they both wanted her gone – you know Easy was into Tinsley.
CelineColista:	Now C's being nice to that slutty Jenny girl, even though she practically had sex with her BF. It's just to piss B off.
BennyCunningham:	God, those bitches are crazy!

OwlNet Instant Message Inbox

SageFrancis:	So Angelica Pardee's marker board got ponied! Do you think?
BennyCunningham:	She's married. And old.
SageFrancis:	Maybe she's secretly wild for Heath . . .
BennyCunningham:	Do you dare me to ask her about it at tonight's check-in?
SageFrancis:	OMG, do it!

A WAVERLY OWL SHOULD NOT CLING TO
THE PAST — ESPECIALLY IF IT'S FULL OF
EX-GIRLFRIENDS.

allie sat in biology class and felt eyes on her that were definitely not welcome. Not the vacant stares of the emaciated dead cats that lay on the metal dissection trays at their lab stations. Brandon Buchanan wouldn't stop staring at her.

It had been almost a year since they'd broken up. She'd gone to a party for Waverly's literary magazine, *Absinthe*, at the library, not intending to break up at all. But the party had been classically romantic — they'd turned the lights down at the library and covered the walls in thick gauzy netting. Old twenties flapper music lilted lightly through the speakers, and everyone had been instructed to wear creative black tie. Easy had been there. She'd known Easy, of course – the eclectic circle of Waverly's elite was small – but not well. She'd always found him sexy and mysterious in a sensitive-artist way, and she'd caught him checking her out a couple of times at chapel. When Brandon went off to get them some drinks, she made eye contact, thinking she'd innocently flirt with Easy from across the room. But then he'd walked up to her. And it had been like those nature shows on PBS, with a lion striking a gazelle. It had happened so fast, she hadn't even known what hit her.

She would've pleaded that Easy had slipped something into her glass, but she hadn't even had a drink yet. Only a few seconds later, they sneaked off into the Waverly ancient-books room, as if they desperately needed to find those dusty tomes of lost John Donne sonnets. Sinking into one of the worn leather smoking chairs, they'd kissed for hours, communicating by telepathy as their tongues twisted together. The next day, Brandon knew – everybody knew – and Callie and Brandon were broken up by lunch.

'By the end of the semester, you will have examined the cat's various bodily systems and identified every organ.' Their handsomely weathered teacher, Mr Shea, paced the room. 'In December you will be given a final oral exam during which you must correctly identify all of the organs.'

From the back of the room, Heath Ferro snickered at the words *oral exam*. Mr Shea switched on the overhead projector and started to point at a line-drawn diagram of a cat. Callie peeked at Brandon again. His eyes remained fixed on her, and she quickly jerked her head away. She doodled,

Stop staring at me, perv, in elaborate cursive on a fresh piece of notebook paper. As soon as she finished the letters, she scribbled over them in broad black strokes.

Suddenly her cell phone vibrated in her back pocket. She slowly took it out, and discreetly slid it onto her lap so that it was obscured by the tabletop. It was a text message from Benny, who was sitting only three rows over.

U think about the cheer yet?

No, Callie texted back.

Every year on Black Saturday, the upperclassmen of the varsity girls' field hockey team performed a cheer. First the whole team would do a really standard and boring cheer. Then it was tradition for the older girls to pick one new younger varsity girl to do another, crazier, sort of embarrassing cheer, having led her to believe that all the girls were doing it together, not just her. Understandably, the girl became completely mortified when she found herself doing the cheer all on her own. Sometimes she wouldn't talk to the other players for weeks. But as the season went on, she invariably laughed about it later, glad to have bonded with the cool older girls. It was a hazing ritual that had started in the fifties, and as co-captain this year, Callie was responsible for it.

Her phone buzzed again. *I think we should make yr new roomie do it*, Benny texted.

Callie froze, her heart leaping in to her throat. No way. Hazing Jenny might make her mad, and Callie had to keep Jenny happy. *I don't think so*, she wrote back. *Is she even varsity?*

Benny buzzed back quickly. *Yup, the list was posted today. Have u seen her play yet? She's kind of all over the place but good.*

Not her, Callie quickly replied.

Callie watched as Benny furiously typed into her tiny Nokia. *But aren't u mad at her b/c of EZ? We can totally embarrass her.*

Callie sat back. The whole school was talking about Jenny and Easy and whispering about Callie as they passed her on the stone pathways around campus. She hadn't told anyone the truth about Easy and Jenny — it was too risky. Embarrassing Jenny was the last thing Callie needed. *I don't know*, she texted back.

Sage and Celine and I all think she's the one to do it. What does Brett think?

As if she and Brett had discussed it. Or anything for that matter. She sighed and dropped her phone into her pale yellow Coach saddle bag, indicating that the conversation was over.

The bell finally rang. Callie jumped up to her feet and grabbed her notebook, hoping that her hair didn't smell like formaldehyde. She felt a hand on her shoulder and turned. It was Brandon, dressed in neatly pressed olive green Zegna trousers and Prada loafers without socks. His hair was flecked with gold and she wondered if he'd used an at-home highlighting kit last night or something. 'Hey,' she greeted him.

'So, easy come, easy go, huh?' Brandon's brown eyes looked cold.

'Pardon?' she asked cautiously.

'How does it feel to have someone steal the one you love out from under you?'

Callie stared at him for a moment and smirked inside. *Good boy, Easy!* He must have already started flirting in public with Jenny. Even before she'd had a chance to tell Jenny about it.

'Well?' Brandon coaxed.

'Yeah, it sucks,' Callie swallowed hard, trying to look heartbroken.

'You don't believe me.' Brandon shrugged. 'But I know something you don't know,' he singsonged.

'What are we, second graders?' she scoffed, suddenly hating how perfectly plucked Brandon's eyebrows were. 'I have to go.'

Shoving past a gaggle of extremely young-looking freshman girls, Callie stopped on the second-floor landing.

Students streamed past her as she pressed herself up against the brick stairwell wall. Was Brandon *still* hoping to get back together with her? Fat chance. That was about as likely as Easy actually falling for little Jenny Humphrey. As if *that* would ever happen.

OwlNet   Instant Message Inbox

RyanReynolds: So, you hear anything on where the Black Saturday party's gonna be? I heard Tinsley's throwing it . . .

CelineColista: Really? I heard she was having a secret love getaway in Lake Como with that guy from Entourage.

RyanReynolds: God, I hope not. I'd die for that girl, she's so hot.

CelineColista: You and every other boy at this school.

RyanReynolds: Try planet.

19

UPON BEING WOOED WITH ROSE PETALS, A WAVERLY OWL SHOULD AT LEAST SAY THANK YOU.

'Hey!' Jeremiah yelled, loping up the long hill from Waverly's practice fields to the main green. Brett squinted. He wore a faded black T-shirt, scruffy beige corduroys and booger-green Pumas. He was smiling so big that Brett could see his crooked row of bottom teeth. Jeremiah probably looked delicious to every other girl on campus, but to Brett, he looked immature and sloppy.

'Hey,' she called, noting the undeniable shakiness in her voice. Jeremiah broke into a run, his floppy red hair flying behind him. He smacked into her and wrapped his strong arms around her waist.

'Babe,' he murmured aggressively. 'It seems like a million *yee-ahs* since I saw you. I feel like we're so *faahhh* from each other.'

Ugh. 'Well, that's silly,' Brett blushed, taking his hand. 'I just talked to you yesterday.'

'You okay?' Jeremiah squeezed her. 'You seem really . . . I don't know. Nervous.'

'Oh, no.' Brett tried to smile. 'I'm just giddy.'

Yeah, she was giddy. But not about Jeremiah. About her mind-blowing, absolutely magical lunch with Mr Dalton. Before she left his office, he'd touched her shoulder and invited her to go to dinner sometime. His nervous, twitching lips when he'd asked, his shining eyes when she'd said yes. Dinner, dinner, dinner with Eric! And they were going *tonight*!

'We're going to the gazebo, right?'

Brett snapped back to attention. 'Yeah,' she squeaked. The old white gazebo was nestled into some weeping willow trees and sat right on the bank of the Hudson. It was a famed Waverly make-out spot – in fact, it was so popular that last spring the students had passed around a gazebo sign-out sheet so nobody would interrupt another couple's business. It had a worn-in, comfy swinging bench for two. There was a cutout hole at the top of the gazebo, so at night, you could look up at the stars. 'But we can't stay too long, 'cause I have to get ready for dinner in a little.'

'That's cool.'

They walked along the stone path, hand in hand, acres

of green lawn and ancient redbrick buildings with bright white trim on either side of them. The sky was getting cloudy, and Brett wasn't sure if it was the humidity or her nerves, but she was definitely sweating a little. Jeremiah suddenly stopped and grabbed her by both hands. Students were walking around campus, heading to the dorms for visiting hours before dinner, all checking out Brett and her hot, floppy-haired boyfriend.

'I really missed you.' He kissed her forehead. 'I wish our schools were closer, you know?'

'They're only about ten miles away from each other,' Brett sputtered, looking around frantically. They were standing right in the middle of the green, in plain view of Stansfield Hall. If Eric looked out his office window right then, he would see them. 'It's really not that far.'

'Well, that seems to far to me.'

'Let's go to the gazebo.' She grabbed his arm quickly. 'We can talk there.'

'Okay.' Jeremiah put his big, snuggly arm around her. 'So, how is it here? You got any freaky new teachers?'

'Um . . .'

'I heard you guys got somebody new. That really rich dude?'

'I don't know . . .' Brett sort of figured all teachers were either really rich and didn't need high-paying jobs or else really poor and desperate.

'Eric Dalton. Have you met him?'

Her heart froze. She glanced at Jeremiah's face. *Was he on to her?*

'Uh . . .'

'You'd know him if you met him. He's a Dalton.'

'What do you mean, he's a *Dalton*?'

Jeremiah looked at her like worms were growing out of her nose. 'Is this just a Massachusetts thing? You know. A Dalton. His grandfather was Reginald Dalton. There's . . . there's like, a giant complex named after him in Boston? The one that always has the big Christmas tree?'

At the Messerschmidts' house in Rumson, there was a picture of four-year-old Brett, wearing a red velvet dress, holding a stuffed Chihuahua, and standing under the Dalton Christmas tree. Duh! *My grandfather was into railroads. My family has a place in Newport.* Eric's words came back to her. She'd never even considered that he was a *Dalton* Dalton.

Brett had watched specials about them on TV, from historical biopics on PBS to scandalous they're-worse-than-the-Kennedys tell-alls on E! She'd learned that the grandfather, Reginald Dalton, was an heir to a railroad fortune. His family owned Lindisfarne, the *largest* mansion in Newport, and had for a hundred years. The father, Morris Dalton, owned an international publishing company that made gazillions of dollars and published only the classiest books and magazines. And yes, she knew there was a son, but he was press-shy and didn't like to be in the spotlight. Brett had assumed he was either ugly or a social misfit or both and that the family's PR secretary wanted to keep him private. How wrong she'd been!

'I think they might've introduced him at chapel,' she finally mumbled to Jeremiah.

'Oh. Well, at least Black Saturday's coming up,' Jeremiah changed the subject, breezing ahead. 'That'll be fun, huh? We've never really partied together, like, during school.'

'Yeah.' Brett took her hand from his, feigning a need to scratch her arm.

'Hey, so close your eyes.' They approached the gazebo. Jerimiah's lacrosse-calloused hand covered the top half of her face. 'I have a surprise.'

He led her a few paces through the grass, breathing excitedly. With every step, Brett felt a heavier and heavier sense of dread. What she really needed was for Jeremiah to go away so she could sit down and think. Eric was Eric *Dalton*? For real?

'Okay, you can open 'em now.' Jeremiah whisked his hand away from her face. Brett gasped. In the middle of the white wooden gazebo was a huge bouquet of black tulips surrounded by heaps of burgundy rose petals. She'd never seen so many flowers in one place before. There must have been a hundred of them.

'I like the black ones,' she squeaked. *Like?* More like she was obsessed with them.

'You said that once when we passed that flower shop in Manhattan.' He beamed, bouncing up and down excitedly, like a little kid who'd just made his parents breakfast in bed.

'I . . .' Brett started. This was the type of thing Callie

always secretly prayed for Easy to do for her, and he never did.

'And here.' Jeremiah held out a white United Airlines envelope. Brett opened it, and saw that it was a first-class round-trip ticket to San Francisco. She looked up at him questioningly.

'My dad is opening up a restaurant on Newbury Street in Boston, and he's going to Sonoma on a tasting tour. He said I could bring you. He'll totally leave us alone, though. It's over Thanksgiving.'

Brett opened her mouth, but nothing came out. Driving through California wine country sounded amazing, but Jeremiah drank beer. She closed her eyes and tried to imagine them together at a winery. You were supposed to spit out the wine after you tasted it, but Jeremiah was the kind of guy who would rather swallow it and get trashed. He was trying too hard. *Way* too hard. Plus Thanksgiving seemed so far away. What if . . . what if she was spending Thanksgiving with Eric?

Hello? They hadn't even kissed yet. But she could still dream . . .

'This is great.' She forced a smile, gazing wondrously at the flowers again.

Jeremiah wrapped his arms around her from behind and kissed her neck softly. 'It was my way of telling you I missed you, baby.'

'Well, it's definitely . . . *something*. I don't know what to say.'

'How about thank you?' Jeremiah's voice sounded a little

edgy all of a sudden, sort of like a scolding mother's.

Brett laughed nervously. 'Okay. Thank you,' she replied, puckering her lips to give him a terse kiss on the cheek.

He turned his head and caught her kiss with his mouth. 'You're most definitely welcome.'

OwlNet

SageFrancis: So I just saw Brett and her hot BF from St Lucius walking toward the gazebo, but she looked miserable. Benny told me she thinks Brett likes someone else. Do u know who?

CallieVernon: Um . . .

SageFrancis: I heard she's been doing some snuggling with a guy between classes.

CallieVernon: A guy from this school? Who?

SageFrancis: Dunno, but he might be older. Like a senior. That's what Benny thinks.

CallieVernon: Huh.

SageFrancis: You didn't know? Are you guys totally fighting or what?

CallieVernon: Kind of. I guess.

OwlNet

To: All New Students
From: DeanMarymount@waverly.edu
Date: Thursday, September 5, 5:01 P.M.
Subject: Welcome!

Dear New Students,

Welcome to Waverly! I hope your first day of classes went well today.

You're invited to an ice cream social for all freshman and transfer students on Friday evening after dinner. The sundae-making will commence at 8:00 P.M. This is a great opportunity to make new friends!

Remember, this is a mandatory event.

Don't worry, I'll bring the sprinkles!

Dean Marymount

A WAVERLY OWL SHOULD RESIST TEMPTATION — ESPECIALLY IF THE TEMPTATION IS HER ROOMMATE'S BOYFRIEND.

L ater that evening, before dinner, it began to pour. Jenny snuggled under the light blue mohair throw her grandmother had knitted for her father when he was at college at Berkeley and read passages of *Madame Bovary* for English class. *The new boy had kept in the background, in the corner behind the door, almost out of sight,* chapter one began. Gloomy tears filled Jenny's eyes. She's read the book last year at Constance Billard and knew it wasn't even about this boy — it was about Emma Bovary, who only wanted to go to parties and sleep with guys who weren't her husband — but still, she empathized with this new bumpkin boy who was being taunted by prep school kids. She wondered if the bumpkin had ever been wrongfully accused and made to choose between popularity and having a big black disciplinary X next to his name.

A key jingled in the door, and Callie burst in, carrying a bunch of shopping bags. Jenny quickly wiped her eyes on the scratchy wool of the throw, making them even redder than they already were.

'Surprise!' Callie sang, pulling a vertical Louis Vuitton signature leather makeup tote out of one of the bags. 'I got new nail polish and a whole bunch of makeup, too. Are you going to be around for a while?'

'Uh, yeah.' Jenny paused, confused. Was Callie talking to her because Brett wasn't here, or was this part of Callie's little suck-up fest? Jenny had gotten another e-gift certificate from Callie that afternoon – $50 to iTunes. It was beginning to feel like the twelve days of Blackmail Christmas.

'Cool.' Callie stopped the CD player – Jenny had been listening to a dreary Yo La Tengo song – and put on Modest Mouse instead. 'So, how was your first day of classes?'

'Um, good,' she responded mechanically, leaning back against the wall behind her bed.

'Look, I just want to thank you for saving my ass from NASCAR High.' Callie giggled, handing Jenny a pint of Ben & Jerry's Phish Food, her favorite. How did she know?

'Well, I mean . . .' Jenny trailed off. 'I didn't say anything, one way or another.'

'I know,' Callie replied gaily. 'And that's okay. You didn't have to say anything to Mr Dalton. When did they say the DC hearing was, anyway?'

'Monday.'

Callie opened her own pint of Phish Food and dug into it with a plastic spoon. She cocked her head and studied Jenny carefully. 'You know, your hair looks really cute like that,' she finally said.

'Are you crazy?' Jenny touched her head. It was raining, and her hair had exploded into a frizz ball. She'd tamed it into a ponytail, but curly wisps were sprouting out everywhere, dancing messily around her face.

'Yeah, I really like it. It's like . . . deconstructed,' she said. 'So, the meeting with Dalton was okay?'

Jenny grunted. 'I guess.'

Callie tried to get a spoonful of ice cream out of the pint container, but the ice cream was too cold and the plastic spoon kept bending. 'So do you think maybe you'll cover for me in DC?'

'Maybe,' Jenny said. 'I'm not—'

'Of course you will,' Callie interrupted. 'And I need you to do me another favor. Well, it's not a favor, really. It'll be fun.'

Jenny stared at her. *Another* favor? Wasn't Callie supposed to be kissing *her* ass? Sure, she hadn't exactly given back the beauty basket or the iTunes gift certificate, but come on!

Callie stabbed her spoon into the ice cream, finally making a dent. 'This might sound a little strange, but I'm wondering if you'll flirt with my boyfriend a little.'

Jenny paused and sucked in her breath. 'You mean . . . Easy?'

'Yeah. It's just, for this to work, it needs to look believ-able that you guys like each other, you know?'

'You want me to . . . flirt?' Jenny repeated.

'Yeah. Like, I don't know. Hang out during dinner. Maybe between classes. Nothing big. Just so teachers can see you.'

Jenny stared at her. She should feel pissed off – flirting with Easy would incriminate her more, wouldn't it? But instead, her heart pounded feverishly.

'You don't want to do it, do you?' Callie's shoulders slumped. 'So he drank a little too much, but he's really sweet once you get to know him.'

'I—'

A knock suddenly sounded on the door. 'Helloooo?' Benny Cunningham cried, bounding into the room. 'Am I interrupting?'

'We're just having some, um, ice cream,' Callie explained quietly. 'I'd offer you some, but it's still too cold.'

'Here's the girl I want to see,' Benny exclaimed, pointing at Jenny.

'Me?' Jenny asked, pointing at herself.

'Yep.' Benny pushed up the sleeves of her Kermit-green thin-gauge cashmere sweater. 'You're playing varsity field hockey, right?'

'Yeah, I made the team today.' Jenny still couldn't believe she was going to play field hockey for Waverly. It was so surreal.

'Great!' Benny squealed. 'We were wondering if you wanted to be part of our Black Saturday cheer. It's usually for upperclassmen, but we pick some younger girls, too. You're a sophomore, right?'

'Yeah.' Jenny looked at Callie. 'Cheer?'

Callie flinched. When Jenny turned her back, Callie mouthed to Benny, *I said I didn't want her.*

Benny ignored her. 'Yeah. It's really fun. We make a new one up every year and torment St Lucius with it. But it's only a certain group of girls, you know?'

'Jeepers.' Jenny's face brightened. 'That sounds really fun.'

'Jeepers?' Benny asked. 'You didn't honestly just say *jeepers*, did you?' She laughed, but Jenny sensed it wasn't actually friendly.

'Um, I mean, cool,' Jenny corrected herself, embarrassed. *Jeepers!* How Old Jenny could she get?

'Yeah?' Benny raised her eyebrows at Callie. Callie scowled back. 'Awesome!'

'Are you doing the cheer too?' Jenny asked Callie.

'Actually, since she's captain, Callie writes the cheer,' Benny explained.

'Really?' Jenny asked curiously. It occurred to her now that being on the field hokey team would be like being in a sorority. She had a whole new family of sisters. It was kind of cool.

Callie swallowed hard. 'I'm working on it.'

'Just get it done before Saturday,' Benny added. 'Okay, so I have to get to the lit mag meeting. Just wanted to make sure Jenny was in. Bye-yee!' She slammed the door shut.

Jenny turned back to Callie. 'You guys do really fun stuff here.'

'Yeah,' Callie answered quietly. 'I wouldn't take it too seriously, though, you know? It's just a stupid cheer.'

Jenny shrugged and licked a tiny bit of too-cold ice cream off her plastic spoon. Slut rumors aside, the cool varsity girls wanted her to do the cheer with them. How cool was that?

The door flew open again and Brett strode in, her blue tweed Eugenia Kim cloche cap soaking wet and her bob-length red hair matted around her face. As soon as she saw them, a peeved look settled over her perfectly chiseled face. 'I thought you guys were both studying tonight.'

'Nope,' Callie replied. 'We're having a makeover-ice cream party.'

'Oh.' Brett threw her cap on the ground.

'Why are you all wet?' Callie asked, sounding much bitchier than necessary.

Brett took off her khaki thigh-length Burberry raincoat and tossed it on the floor. 'Jeremiah was here. We got stuck in the rain.'

'Jeremiah?' Callie straightened up, thinking about the IM she'd received from Sage earlier. 'Did you guys have the big talk?'

Brett looked at her blankly. 'Big talk? We . . . whatever. We hung out.'

Callie stared back, a half-smirk on her face. *Come on.* They were best friends. If Brett liked some other guy, surely she'd tell Callie about it. There were plenty of hot seniors at this school – Parker DuBois, for instance. Parker was half French, had large, piercing blue eyes, and was a photography ingénue, having spent the summer snapping shots of edgy, upcoming artists for the *New York Times* Sunday Fashion supplement. Callie could totally see Brett liking Parker. She waited, locking her hazel eyes with Brett's green ones, until Brett silently looked down.

'Who's Jeremiah?' Jenny broke the silence.

'I guess Jeremiah is Brett's boyfriend.' Callie tried to catch Brett's eye again but couldn't. She sighed. 'He's gorgeous and athletic and sweet and throws the best parties at St Lucius.'

'Jeepers,' Jenny couldn't help exclaiming again, trying to hide her surprise. From the fawning way Brett had been acting in the meeting this morning with Mr Dalton in his office, Jenny had just assumed she was single.

'Why didn't you bring him over to the room?' Callie asked. 'Or did you guys just do it in the rain in the middle of the practice fields?'

Jenny watched Callie talk at Brett. She was doing that thing some people do when they act nice and chipper and interested, while just below the surface they're thinking really mean thoughts, and you can never call them on it because they'd just accuse you of being paranoid.

Brett rolled her eyes. 'No, we didn't do it anywhere. Why would anyone want to do it in a field? Gross. Do you and Easy do it in a field? Did you and Brandon do it in a field?' Brett stormed over to her closet and hung up her coat.

'Whoa. Someone's PMSing,' Callie scoffed, examining her nails.

Jenny was still thinking about how Brett had flirted with Mr Dalton when she heard Brandon's name. 'Did she say Brandon?' Jenny asked Callie. 'Like, Brandon Buchanan?'

'Yeah. I went out with him for almost a year. He didn't tell you that?'

'No.'

'Huh. I thought he told everybody. One time last winter, a whole bunch of us went to Park City to snowboard, and Brandon met a group of Swiss tourists and told them every detail of our tortured relationship, even though we'd already broken up by that point. And then he pleaded with me all night to go into the sauna with him.'

Jenny wrinkled her nose. That didn't sound like Brandon at all.

Callie shook her head. 'I know. Hello? Saunas are so germy. Nobody goes into them except old gay men.'

'Saunas are fine, Callie,' Brett contradicted from her closet. 'Easy went in the sauna on that trip.'

Callie blushed and drew in her bottom lip. 'Anyway,' she whispered to Jenny, 'where were we? Oh. Easy. So, what do you think?'

'Well, I guess . . .' Jenny began. She sort of wanted to ask, *Will me flirting with him freak Easy out*? But maybe that was an Old Jenny question. And he had touched New Jenny's back . . .

'What are you talking about?' Brett demanded, stepping out of her closet.

'Nothing!' Jenny and Callie responded in unison.

'Awesome,' Callie continued, turning back to Jenny. 'It'll be fun. Easy's sweet. And it'll all be over soon.'

Jenny bit her lip. Not too soon, she hoped.

21

A WAVERLY OWL SHOULD BE TRUE TO HER ROOTS.

few minutes later, after the rain cleared and the late-summer sky began to turn a faded orange, students walked in cliquish groups from their dorms to the dining hall, and Brett strode down the stone path toward Waverly's front office. A crisp wind suddenly lifted the edges of her dove-gray sheer silk Hermès scarf, which made Brett think of winter. Most kids hated winter at Waverly, because you were stuck indoors and there was nothing to do except watch old films at the library and go to class. But Brett loved it. The dorm mistresses lit fires in the common rooms, and the teachers canceled classes on the first day of snow. By four it was already dark, and she and Callie would drink peppermint schnapps-spiked hot cocoa while they gossiped about their latest crushes. Brett was pretty sure she wasn't going to be drinking cocoa with Callie this winter – they were barely talking – but maybe she'd have someone else to drink cocoa with. Naked.

As she sidestepped a couple of fat brown squirrels fighting over a Cheeto, Brett's cell phone beeped with a text message. *Sorry we got cut off before*, it said. *Luv you, Sissy!*

Brett quickly called Bree back and got her voice mail. 'I'm about to go out to dinner with a *Dalton*,' she whispered delightedly into her phone. 'Be jealous. Be very jealous.' Then she pressed end.

Brett entered the front office, a giddy, sour feeling festering in the pit of her stomach. The lobby was empty, and *The New Yorker*, *The Economist* and *National Geographic* were arranged neatly on the huge teak coffee table. A Vivaldi symphony was playing over the stereo. The old cherry floors squeaked under her three-inch black Jimmy Choo boots as Brett approached the fiftyish front desk attendant, Mrs Tullington.

'I need a pass for the night,' Brett said casually. And, because you always needed an appropriate reason: 'I'm accompanying my uncle to a silent auction of ancient Russian artifacts and Fabergé eggs in Hudson.'

Brett knew that a lie sounded more convincing when you threw in a whole bunch of ridiculous details.

Mrs Tullington eyed Brett over her tortoiseshell-rimmed glasses. The wrinkles around her mouth puckered in disapproval. Brett wore a black chalk-striped, slit-down-the-side Armani skirt. Her Vincent Longo-painted lips were bright red, her pale arms were bare, and the V in her black silk shell top was so low you could almost see her black lace Eres bra.

Finally Mrs T. wrote out the pass. 'Enjoy the eggs,' she said primly. 'And your uncle. Nice that you girls stay close with family.'

The thing was, if Mrs T. had bothered to look out the building's bay window, she would have seen Brett get into a hunter green '57 Jaguar — a car that most definitely did not belong to Brett's uncle, a fortyish out-of-work-actor-cum-personal-trainer who worked out flabby new moms at the Body Electric gym in Paramus. Eric wore dark blue pressed True Religion jeans and a crisp tucked-in white button-down. Brett covered her knees with her skirt, feeling slightly overdressed.

'You look nice.' Eric grinned, gripping the gearshift sexily.

'Oh. Thanks.'

A Sigur Rós song played on the Bose CD player. The windows were down, and a cool late-summer breeze wafted in. As they swept down Waverly's front hill past the practice fields, Brett felt a sudden, disorienting thrill. Maybe they were leaving the school for good — and never coming back. *Suckers*. She thought about everyone else sitting down to dinner right now at the dining hall. On Thursdays it was pasta with watery tomato sauce and nasty fried chicken.

She snuck a peek at Eric's profile — his slightly upturned nose and perfect, just-stubbly-enough jaw — and then stared down at the platinum-engraved gate-link bracelet he wore on his right wrist. It seemed like something a girl might have given him.

'It's my great-great grandfather's,' he explained, noticing her stare. He jiggled the bracelet around his wrist. 'Like it?'

'Yes,' she answered breathlessly. The bracelet was practically an American treasure. 'It's beautiful.'

They drove out of Waverly territory and into town, essentially one main street with quaint little wrought-iron street lamps, an art store, a florist, a barbershop with the swirly pole, and a few brick Federal-style houses. Brett figured they were going to Le Petit Coq. It was the place that your family always dragged you to during Parents' Weekend because it was haughty and French and the only place for miles that served foie gras. But the Jag breezed right by without slowing down. It sped by the strip mall just outside of town, past McDonald's and the cineplex, too.

'I guess I should've asked.' Eric turned to Brett. 'How late did you sign out for?'

'Midnight,' Brett said. It was six o'clock now.

Eric smiled. 'That gives us six hours.'

He pulled into a spacious parking lot, drove through an alley, and then swung around a large, concrete squat building. It was the Waverly airport, the place she'd flown into on her parents' small plane a couple of days ago. On the runway sat a perky little Piper Cub. A man in a green bomber jacket and a Boston Red Sox ball cap stood chewing on an unlit cigar on the runway beside the plane. He waved and Eric waved back.

'Where are we going?' Brett demanded. Her heart beat quickly. She didn't know what to expect, but she knew enough to be excited. If this outing involved an airplane — she couldn't imagine where they might go. Holy fucking shit!

Eric shut off the car's engine. 'I was thinking maybe we could get something better than the early bird special at the Little Rooster.'

'Going to Lindisfarne?' the guy in the bomber called.

'That's right,' Eric called back.

Of course. They were going to his family's estate in Newport. Brett could hardly contain herself. This was like that cheesy movie, *The Princess Diaries.* Except she was way cooler than that mousy Anne Hathaway, and he was a Dalton!

Brett had only seen Lindisfarne on the *E! True Hollywood* special, so when the Piper Cub touched down on the property's runway, a glittery, unreal feeling washed over her. The oceanfront mansion was an ivy-covered stone castle, with turrets and a moat and everything. She even remembered from the E! special that rare trumpeter swans swam in the moat surrounding the mansion instead of alligators, although Brett didn't see swans now. Maybe they were sleeping. And as she stepped off the plane onto the spongy, perfectly mani-cured lawn, even the salty ocean air felt regal. It took Brett and Eric nearly ten minutes to walk from the landing strip to the manor. They were greeted by the groundskeeper's friendly, rotund yellow lab, Mouse, before he was called off by his owner in the distance, who waved at Eric.

First Eric showed her around the property, taking her into the house through one of the heavy dark oak front doors and into the French room, which was round, with a high rotunda and white scalloped detailing. Brett could barely breathe. Everything in her life that might come after this moment – say, getting into any Ivy League school or moving into a Tribeca loft or meeting the president of France – would pale in comparison to standing in the stately blue French room, admiring the large, blurry Monets on the walls.

Brett was so overwhelmed, she could barely focus as he led her from room to room. Then he guided her back outside to the guest house, a weathered green cottage with a huge back deck and wooden stairs to the ocean. Most guest houses consisted of a bedroom and a small living space. The Lindsfarne guest house was nearly the size of Brett's parents' not-at-all-small house. Inside, Brett sat in an oversized chintz sofa, gazing the white, Warhol-covered walls as Eric fussed around in the kitchen. If the Daltons had staff – and she was sure they had many – they certainly knew when to leave the members of the family alone.

Eric expertly poured 1980 L'Evangile Bordeaux into both of their oversized Riedel glasses. He didn't seem to care that Brett was blatantly underage. 'This is where I live, mostly, when I'm here,' he explained, swirling the wine in his glass as they stepped outside onto the wraparound wooden deck.

Only a few feet away, waves crashed against the rocks. Brett took a big gulp of wine. What a life.

'So,' Eric began. 'Brett Messerschmidt. What are you all about?'

He looked at her not in that way adults do when they think you're a silly teenager who may grow up and be somebody serious. Instead, he looked at her intensely, as if she really *mattered*. Brett took a sip of wine, desperately trying to think of a brilliant but succinct answer. Who was Brett Messerschmidt?

'Well, I like Dorothy Parker,' she replied, and then wanted to smack herself for sounding like a stuck-up, lame, immature *student*.

'Really?' he asked, biting his lip as if to say, *That really wasn't what I wanted to know*. 'What else? Tell me something about your family.'

'My family?' she gulped, the words seizing up in her throat. It was probably the worst question Eric could ask. She felt her cheeks turning red. 'I don't really like to talk about them.'

'Why?' He took a sip of wine. 'Can I venture a guess?'

She shrugged. 'Go for it.' She hoped she seemed unruffled, even though she was freaking out inside.

'Your parents treat you like a princess. You're spoiled rotten.'

Brett took another big sip of wine. 'I suppose,' she said warily. 'Aren't you?'

Eric smiled. 'I suppose.'

'But yes, to answer your question, yes, I was spoiled,' Brett began. Her fake family story about living on an organic farm in East Hampton and throwing benefits for endangered birds sat on the tip of her tongue, ready, but she stopped. Something about the way Eric was looking at her made her feel like maybe she could tell him the truth, as embarrassing as it was. She was filled with a sense of calm. 'My parents' house . . . my mother modeled it after Versailles,' she began slowly. 'Except it's in . . . well, Rumson, New Jersey.'

'I know Rumson,' Eric cut in. 'I sailed by there a couple of times. It looks like a nice place to grow up.'

Brett eyed him carefully. He didn't seem to be making fun of her. She took another sip of wine and then a big breath.

'You've probably seen my parents' house, then,' she went on. 'It's the biggest one on the shore. My parents are kind of like the *Sopranos*. You know how they're all dripping with money but just use it in really stupid ways? That's them. Except they're legal. And have less taste, if that's possible.'

'So your mother's favorite pattern is leopard print?' Eric goaded.

'Oh, much worse. Zebra. On everything. Stretch pants. Socks. Bar stools. It's gross. My sister — she's a fashion editor — has threatened many times to secede from our family.'

Eric chuckled. 'My mother likes paisleys. They look like little sperms.'

'Ew!' Brett squealed.

She felt dizzy, although she'd had less than a glass of wine. Talking about her parents with Eric didn't feel weird at all. She wondered why she'd thought, all these years, that things would be better if she had a normal-size grey-shingled Cape Cod and a couple of Toyotas instead of twin gold Hummers with matching zebra-print leather interiors and big gold M's (for Messerschmidt) embroidered on the headrests. Opening up this much was infectious. She wanted to keep going.

'My mother wears pink diamonds and eats only Lindt truffles and Zoloft, and has seven teensy, tiny Teacup Chihuahuas with matching zebra collars. She carries them everywhere. And my dad, he's a plastic surgeon.' It all came rushing out of Brett. She couldn't believe the things she was telling Eric.

'Really.' Eric rested his chin on the heel of his hand. 'Tell me more.'

'Okay,' she continued eagerly. 'Sometimes at dinner Dad has these famous clients over, and they talk about really disgusting things. Like what their boobs looked like before the surgery. And what happens to all of the fat that they suck out of people.' She felt liberated. It was like skinny-dipping.

Eric leaned forward. 'So what *do* they do with it?'

'They use cells from it,' she whispered. 'You know, for research.'

'From *fat*?' he whispered back, sounding sort of appalled.

She nodded. 'Well, um, yeah, but sometimes they just throw it away.'

He leaned back and looked at her carefully with a bemused grin on his face. 'God, that's refreshing.'

'Refreshing?'

He shifted in his seat and stared out at the water. A small, graceful white sailboat bobbed out in front of the guest house, maybe 500 feet from the shore. 'Everyone's always trying to talk themselves up – even the kids at Waverly, who are a lot more privileged than most. I mean, nobody is just honest about who they are and who their family is. Who cares if your dad won the Nobel Prize or if he sucked fat out of some Jersey woman's ass? What does that have to do with you?'

She stared at him. 'Yeah,' she agreed. 'It's so true.'

He stared back at her. 'You're different,' he concluded.

Brett met his gaze, and everything inside her felt like it was about to explode. 'Will you excuse me?' She cleared her throat. 'I have to make a phone call.'

'Sure.' Eric tipped his chair back and, as she stood, he ever so lightly touched her left hip. She paused for a second as her hair dipped into her eyes. His hand lingered there. Then a grandfather clock from some far-off room sounded and he pulled away.

She stepped out onto the dewy grass, lit a cigarette, and teetered up the steps of a wooden gazebo surrounded by lilacs. She breathed in the sweet scent, willing herself not to lose her nerve. She dialed, and after a single ring, Jeremiah's voice mail picked up. 'Yo, I'm not hee-ah. Leave a message, losah!' *Beep.*

'It's Brett,' she blurted hoarsely, seething at the sound of his thuggish recording. 'I don't think we should see each other anymore. So, um, don't stay around for the Black Saturday party after the game. I can't explain right now, but it's what I want. I'm, um, really sorry. 'Bye.'

Brett stepped back onto the grass. Eric had wandered

out of the house and was absentmindedly swirling cognac in a snifter, his dark jeans rolled up to his knees. The vast sky was dark and purple, and tiny lights twinkled out on the water. She could hear waves lapping on the shore and the gentle groan of a far-off foghorn.

'Everything all right?' he asked, grabbing her cigarette to take a drag.

She nodded. Then, wordlessly, he pointed out to the green twinkly light in the middle of the sound.

'That's my boat. I don't have class on Fridays, so I was thinking of sailing it up to Waverly.'

'I like the little green light,' Brett mused. 'It reminds me of *The Great Gatsby* – you know, when Gatsby would look out to Daisy's dock for the light to be on?'

'Sure,' he said. 'Maybe I'll have to leave the light on sometimes when I dock at school.'

Brett tried not to smile. 'Who do you think will be looking for it?' she asked. But from the look on his face, Brett suspected he meant it for one very special girl from Rumson, New Jersey.

22

ART CLASS IS THE BEST PLACE FOR
WAVERLY OWLS TO TELL SECRETS.

Portraiture class met only twice a week, on Tuesdays and Fridays, and Jenny had been eagerly anticipating the first class of the year. Waverly had a stellar art program and a glass-walled riverfront gallery with student-curated public shows. Often student pieces even sold for surprising sums. Normally you had to submit work to be accepted to portraiture class, but since Jenny had been admitted to Waverly on the strength of her art portfolio, she'd been allowed into the class her first semester. Art was her favorite subject and she couldn't wait to smell the paint and lose herself in the process of making something new.

And yes, seeing Easy Walsh would be pretty exciting

too. Especially now that she had permission to flirt with him!

The class was in a building called Jameson House, a rambling country cottage with blue clapboard siding, a stone chimney, and a clothesline outside of tie-dyed American flags from one of last year's fabric-making projects. Inside, the unfinished floors creaked, and all sorts of random drawings and half-finished color studies were pinned up to the whitewashed wall. The four giant rooms smelled like turpentine, aerosol fixative, wet clay, and the old-fashioned wood-fired kiln. Jenny stood inside, breathing it in.

'Welcome, welcome,' called Mrs Silver, her art teacher. She was doughy and huggable, with pale, ample arms and gray hair piled on the top of her head in an enormous messy bun. She wore a whole bunch of bangle bracelets on her left wrist, giant oversized green and yellow striped overalls, and an extra-large tie-dyed rainbow T-shirt she'd definitely made herself.

The room had sloping ceilings, slanted art desks, and a wall of cathedral-size windows pouring in light. Mrs Silver's desk was a mess of paintbrushes, old leaded glass bottles, little aromatherapy vials, thick coffee-table art books, yoga flash cards, and a two-liter jug of Mountain Dew. Mrs Silver was messier than Jenny's father. She bet the two of them would really hit it off.

'Oh, Easy!' Mrs Silver called. 'I'm so happy to see you! Did you have a lovely summer?'

Jenny turned. Easy Walsh strode up to Mrs Silver and kissed her tenderly on her cheek. Today his Waverly jacket was slung over his arm, and he wore a mustard-yellow T-shirt with frayed edges and medium-gray Levi's that fit his muscular butt perfectly. His wavy hair was all over the place, and Jenny noticed that a little yellow maple leaf was tucked behind his right ear.

Easy scanned the classroom. His pale blue eyes lingered on her for a second. Jenny realized that the only empty desk in the classroom was right next to hers.

'Okay, everyone,' Mrs Silver announced. 'Let's get right to it, because I know you kids are eager. I'm passing out sketch paper and mirrors now. We'll start on rough sketches of our self-portraits.'

A collective groan rose up. Self-portraits were the worst.

Easy slowly walked to the desk next to Jenny's, his eyes focused on her the whole time. He threw his cracked tan leather knapsack under the desk and sat down on the adjacent short metal stool. Then he slowly unraveled his Bose headphones from his neck and wrapped the cord around his slim white iPod. He leaned over and wrote on Jenny's desk with a stub of charcoal, *Hey*. His handwriting was boyish and spiky.

Hello, Jenny wrote right underneath it in elegant calligraphy.

Mrs Silver handed out charcoal, Prismacolor markers, mirrors, and rolls of shelf paper to each student. Jenny stared at her reflection. Her eyes belied the sea of nerves inside of her. *It's okay*, she told herself. *Callie told you to flirt*. But had Callie told her to have heart palpitations?

'So, did Dalton give you a hard time?' Easy whispered.

'Not really,' Jenny whispered back. She wondered if Callie had told him that she hadn't made a decision about whether to take the blame or not yet.

'Is Callie giving you a hard time?'

'Callie? Uh, no . . .' Jenny put the blunt end of her marker in her mouth. 'She's been okay.'

'Well, I hope she's not putting you through too much shit. She does that sometimes.'

Jenny wondered what that meant. She turned back to her blank sketch paper, well aware that Easy seemed to be sneaking glances at her out of the corner of his eye. Before Old Jenny could stop her and tell her that even though Callie had said she *could* flirt, she shouldn't, New Jenny giggled and poked Easy with her Prismacolor marker, leaving a big red mark on his forearm.

'What was that for?' he whispered, examining the mark.

'I wanted to give you a tattoo.' She decided that the mark was a nose and added two tiny eyes and a mouth.

'It's beautiful,' he declared. Then, he grabbed his own blue Prismacolor and wrote on her arm, *HI JENNY*, and drew a frowning, snaggletoothed cartoon character, complete with a curly sprig of hair on the top of its head.

'Is it a portrait of me?' Jenny laughed.

'No . . . is yours a portrait of me?'

'Nooo. But, I once painted my boyfriend in six different styles, from Pollock to Chagall.'

'My dad has a Chagall in his study,' Easy told her. 'It looks kind of like *I and the Village*. I used to stare at that painting for hours when I was little.'

Jenny blinked, caught off guard. *I and the Village* was her favorite. 'You . . . you had great taste for a kid.'

'So, are you still with this boyfriend?' Easy murmured, shyly turning away as he said it and looking carefully into his own little handheld mirror. He made bold charcoal strokes on the blank page in front of him. It was exciting to watch him draw.

'Oh, no,' Jenny answered quickly. She and Nate had only been together for about three weeks, and then he'd totally blown her off on New Year's Eve. He was older and had probably just been using her to get back at his real girl-friend.

'You must've liked him, though. You painted him six times.'

Jenny shadowed an area around her self-portrait's nose, reviewing the slight lie in her head before she said it out loud. 'Well, he liked me more than I liked him.'

'I'm sure,' Easy said softly.

Jenny sucked in her breath and took another peek at his adorable profile. As she switched charcoals, she saw him peek at her, too. So it wasn't exactly right, but she couldn't stop herself. Besides, it was what Callie had asked her to do, wasn't it?

'So Jenny, you know any good secrets?'

Her hand slipped and made a big black wiggly line across her portrait's cheek. How about Brett coming in at 3 A.M. after Jenny had seen her leave campus with Mr Dalton earlier that night? That was a pretty big secret. There was also the gigantically real crush Jenny had on

Easy – another juicy one. 'Um, not really,' she responded quietly.

'I do,' Easy offered.

Jenny felt her heart thud in her throat. 'What is it?'

He lowered his eyes, then looked at her again. 'I'll write it down, but you have to read it later.'

'Why can't you say it?'

'Because it's a secret.' He scribbled something in charcoal on a piece of scrap paper, folded it three times, and handed it to her.

Jenny took the note and shoved it into her pocket. Then something suddenly occurred to her. Callie had briefed her on how she should flirt with Easy, but maybe Callie had told Easy the exact same thing. *Just be nice to Jenny: hang out with her a little, make it look like you guys like each other.* Jenny could totally see that happening.

Her heart sank. Was that it, and nothing more?

As soon as the bell rang, she rushed into the first stall of the Jameson House girls' room and opened the note. In chicken-scratched, blurry charcoal letters it said:

The owls at Waverly talk. Maybe they'll talk to us together sometime.

Jenny creased the note into smaller and smaller folds and shoved it in her bag. There was no denying that she had a full-on crush on Easy Walsh. Everything about him, from his dark messy hair to his sumptuous, uneven mouth, to his love of Chagall, to his navy-blue-ink-stained hands.

She finally emerged from the stall and stared into the smeared sink mirror. She didn't know what she was looking for – maybe evidence, like a physical sign, that something monumental was happening.

Because she was pretty sure Easy was honestly flirting with her. Not because Callie had told him to but because he wanted to. She wasn't sure how she knew, but she *knew*.

OwlNet

Email Inbox

To: BrettMesserschmidt@waverly.edu
From: EricDalton@waverly.edu
Date: Friday, September 6, 3:33 P.M.
Subject: Fw: Upcoming Disciplinary Committee hearing

Brett,

I'm forwarding you this e-mail from Marymount, below, since it's about the upcoming DC hearing. Thought you should know.

And thank you for joining me for dinner last night. It was very . . . refreshing.

See you soon,

EFD

Begin forwarded message:

To: EricDalton@waverly.edu
From: DeanMarymount@waverly.edu
Date: Friday, September 6, 2:20 A.M.
Subject: Upcoming Disciplinary Committee hearing

Dear Eric,

As you know, the first DC case of the year, involving Easy Walsh and Jennifer Humphrey, is scheduled for Monday. I'd like to make sure we set a no-tolerance precedent with this case.

However, Mr Walsh is a legacy and his parents are donors, which obviously causes some complications. It's a shame, because I personally reviewed Miss Humphrey's application and think she's a terrific addition to the Waverly art program, but someone has to take the fall for this. If she's found guilty, I'm afraid we'll have to expel her.

Let's make sure we start the year off on the right foot.

Thanks in advance,

Dean Marymount

23

IN MATTERS OF SPORT, A WAVERLY OWL
SHOULD ALWAYS BE A TEAM PLAYER.

Friday afternoon, Brett sat in the locker room before the first day of field hockey practice tugging at the silver Tiffany *étoile* ring Jeremiah had given her over the summer. The thing was stuck on her finger, but she wanted it off. As soon as she'd sunk into the plush black leather seats of Eric's family limousine – he'd had a car take her back to Waverly since he was sailing back in his boat – she'd been in Eric withdrawal. They hadn't even kissed, but she felt like she could still smell him on her. That delicious Acqua di Parma. And this morning's café au lait had tasted like L'Evangile Bordeaux.

'Hey,' a voice beckoned shyly.

Brett turned to see Jenny sitting next to her on the long,

forest-green bench, pulling socks over her shin guards. Her wild brown hair was pulled back off her face in a high pony-tail, and she wore gray Champion sweat shorts and a cutoff lavender-colored T-shirt with an orange Les Best logo, which was an edgy, preppy-girl-goes-crazy label based in Manhattan's Meatpacking District. Brett had felt bad for Jenny when she received Eric's e-mail, but that was what you got for getting in bed with Callie . . . and Easy. 'Hey,' Brett said back.

Jenny squirmed, pretzeling her legs, as if she had to pee. 'So, I think there's something you should know.'

Brett stared at Jenny. Was she going to fess up about what had happened that night with Easy? Or maybe Callie had confessed something about Tinsley's expulsion? Whatever it was, Brett definitely wanted to hear it. 'What?'

'I . . . I saw you get in. In the middle of the night. And I know where you were.'

Brett stared at her, feeling her lips curl up the way they did when she got scared. '*What?*' Her voice was barely audible.

'It's okay,' Jenny said quickly. Brett's face grew paler and paler, making her eyes look huge and dark. Jenny had contemplated whether or not it made sense to say anything to Brett. The thing was, Jenny wasn't so great at keeping secrets. She wasn't someone who would tell the whole world, but she always had to tell at least one other person. It made carrying the secret's burden a little easier. So why not tell Brett's secret back to Brett?

'You don't know anything,' Brett muttered, turning away to look at the freshly raked playing field.

'Look, please, *please* don't worry,' Jenny pleaded, her voice growing squeaky. 'Your secret is safe with me. Honestly. Maybe I shouldn't have said anything.'

From the middle of the field, Coach Smail blew the whistle. 'Girls! Gather around!'

Brett stared at Jenny. Was she serious, or was this some sort of ploy? Could Jenny be trusted? Last year Brett and Callie and Tinsley used to sit around in their room at night and talk about every detail of their days, no matter how mundane or spectacular. They'd been the kind of best friends who are almost like sisters, because they loved one another so much that even when they pissed each other off, they knew they were still going to be each other's bridesmaids someday. But the Tinsley/E fiasco had made Brett a lot more suspicious. If Callie could betray Tinsley like that — not that Brett knew exactly what had gone down, but still — who knew what she would do to Brett?

'You better not tell anybody,' Brett warned, ignoring Jenny's annoyingly innocent expression. She couldn't possibly be that innocent, especially if she was from the city.

'Look, as far as I'm concerned, we never had this conversation,' Jenny insisted loyally. 'But . . . I just want to make sure . . . Are you okay? 'Cause you seem, like, a little distracted.'

Brett gripped her hockey stick and stood up. No one ever asked her if she was okay, not even her parents, and she wasn't sure how to answer. 'Um, I don't know. Can I get back to you on that?'

Jenny smiled eagerly. 'Sure. See ya!' She picked up her stick and jogged toward the middle of the field, where the team was waiting.

'Hey!' Brett called. Jenny turned, and Brett noticed that weird, familiar glimmer about Jenny again – like she was channeling Tinsley, like they had the same special something seeping out of their tiny pores.

Jenny turned to find Brett jogging toward her. 'Look, whatever happened with you and, um, Easy?' Brett said quietly. 'Well, I shouldn't tell you this, but Marymount wants to make an example of you, to, like, set a precedent for the year. So . . . I'll try my hardest to keep you from getting expelled, but, well, I don't know what's going to happen.'

'Oh.' Jenny's shoulders slumped. *Expelled?* 'Um, thanks.'

Celine Colista, who had olive skin, straight black hair, and full lips coated with MAC Rabid lipstick, ran up to them, kicking up grass behind her with her cleats. 'Jenny, did Callie give you the cheer yet?'

Jenny shook her head.

'Cheer?' Brett asked.

'Yeah. Jenny is going to be part of our *cheer*,' Celine explained very slowly.

Brett nodded uneasily. Then Celine turned back to Jenny. 'C'mon. Let's go talk to Callie.'

Callie was sitting on the long metal bench alongside the field, rewrapping her field hockey stick with tape. She looked up just in time to see Celine and Jenny running over. *Shit.*

Benny and Celine just weren't going to let this cheer thing die.

'Callie,' Celine cooed. 'Did you write the words yet?'

'I'm working on it.'

'Well, you have to hurry!' Celine whined. 'Okay, fine, we can finish them at the party tonight.' Celine winked at Callie and then trotted to center field.

Jenny turned to Callie. 'Party?'

'Yeah,' Callie replied, looking down at her field hockey stick. 'It's a pre-Black Saturday thing. Girls only. You have to come. We all dress up!'

'As what?'

'Well, it's a secret until the last minute. But it's tonight, probably in Dumbarton's upstairs common room.'

'Tonight?' Jenny looked crestfallen. 'I have to go to a new students' ice cream social thing tonight.'

'Whatever. You can get out of that.'

'No, the e-mail said it was mandatory.' Jenny shrugged. 'I should probably go. But I'm really excited about Black Saturday. There's a secret party then too, right? And this cheer sounds cool.'

'Well, the cheer's so not a big deal. You don't have to do it if you don't want to.'

'No, I do!' Jenny couldn't keep the shakiness out of her voice. The girls were all talking to her, and she felt more included than she ever had before, but she was also about to be expelled.

Callie was tempted to confess that the cheer was a not-very-funny joke, but a few years ago, when Tasha Templeton, then the captain of the team, had told the new girl, Kelly Bryers, she was about to be punk'd, the whole team had unleashed on her. They'd cut holes in her bras, right where the nipples were. And no one had spoken to her for months. Her boyfriend had broken up with her, and she'd lost all her power. Callie didn't dare.

Suddenly, Callie looked down at Jenny's skinny arms and noticed the letters peeking out from underneath her right sleeve. It looked like Jenny had scrubbed at her arm for a while to get the marker off, but Callie could still make out the familiar boyish, messy script, and that stupid spiky-toothed face that Easy always drew. Immediately, a knot formed in her stomach, and she felt the hair on the back of her neck rise. *What was Easy doing writing on this bitch's arm?* But then she stopped herself. *Chill. You asked him to do this.*

'So how's Easy?' she inquired instead, swallowing her worry.

'Oh,' Jenny squeaked.

'You getting along all right?'

'Uh, yeah.'

'Good.' With any luck, the teachers would think so too. But why was Easy writing stuff on Jenny's arm? That wasn't really necessary. Especially that snaggletoothed character of his. That was her character: they'd made it up that time they snuck down to Brooklyn and spent the whole day in Williamsburg, shopping for vintage clothes and avant-garde art. They'd gone to Schiller's Liquor Bar on the Lower East Side after that, and he'd drawn the silly face right onto the back of the menu. Then they'd snuck into the tiny bathroom and kissed, annoying all the impatient French tourists.

All Callie had wanted was a little flirting, and, as usual, Easy had gone overboard. But *whatever*. If it meant Jenny would take the fall for her at DC, then Jenny could have the snaggletoothed dude.

'Come on.' She squeezed Jenny's arm, trying her hardest not to appear jealous. 'Smail's giving us the evil eye.'

OwlNet   Email Inbox

To: EasyWalsh@waverly.edu
From: CallieVernon@waverly.edu
Date: Friday, September 6, 4:15 P.M.
Subject: Miss you!

Hi Sweetheart,

I miss you! Please meet me at the library steps at 5 P.M. today.
Sharp!

xoxoxoxxox,
C

P.S. How's Jenny?

```
 ___
(o o)   OwlNet                           Email Inbox
 \_/
```

To: JenniferHumphrey@waverly.edu
From: CustomerCare@rhinecliffwoods.com
Date: Friday, September 6, 4:23 P.M.
Subject: Spa treatment

Dear Jenny Humphrey,

Callie Vernon has sent you a gift certificate for a relaxing spa treatment at our facilities. You're all signed up for a shiatsu massage and an oxygen-blast facial. Please call or e-mail to schedule your appointment.

Regards,

Bethany Bristol

Rhinecliff Woods Spa Manager

**WAVERLY OWLS MUST USE THE
RARE-BOOK ROOM FOR STUDYING ONLY.**

'I can't see,' Easy mumbled, as Callie led him blind-folded up the smooth marble stairs of the library. 'That's the point. I want to surprise you.'

She pushed through the unmarked, heavy oak door. Beyond it were walls and walls of books, glass cases of scrolls, leather smoking chairs, and a tiny, Mondrian-patterned stained-glass window. *So* romantic. She pulled her hands away from his eyes.

'The library?' He looked around, confused.

'Not just the library.' She folded up the red satin eye mask she'd gotten from flying first class on Iberia. 'Don't you remember? It's the rare-book room! It's where we first . . .' She trailed off, pushing a lock of blond hair behind her shoulder. What to say? Where they first consummated their love? They hadn't consummated anything. They'd made out. She'd put her hand on the outside of his pants. She'd cheated on her then-boyfriend, Brandon.

'Yeah, I realize that,' Easy replied, walking around the room, running his hands over a row of rare, dusty books. There were first-edition Steinbeck, Faulkner, and Hemingway novels in a large glass case, thanks to a certain J. L. Walsh and an R. Dalton. There were four large Rothkos on the wall, all of them studies in different-size black and red squares.

Callie sat down on one of the leather chairs. It was cold against the backs of her legs, and she immediately got goose-bumps. 'Maybe we could reenact that night?' she said softly, pulling at Easy's pale gray T-shirt. 'Here, why don't you get comfortable?'

She stood and gently pushed Easy into a brown leather club chair. She sat in his lap and started kissing his neck. Easy slid his hand under her paper-thin TSE white T-shirt and fingered her white de la Renta bra.

This was *perfect*. The musty smell of the old books, the sensual glow of the Tiffany stained-glass lamp in the corner, the stillness of everything. Callie felt like she was being naughty in her father's reading room, or like she was a frustrated baroness from the 1700s who was getting a little action before they all had high tea. It seemed like something out of a D. H. Lawrence novel. *Women in Love*, maybe.

Then she noticed that Easy's eyes were open. Wide open.

'What?' she asked, pulling back.

'I think that's a first-edition of *V*,' he murmured, leaning forward to get a better look. 'I didn't notice it here before . . .'

Callie let out a frustrated little squeal and pulled her knees up to her chin, cuffing Easy in the jaw as she did.

'What?' Easy shot back.

'Never mind,' she said quietly, realizing that the hurt in her voice was coming through way more than she wanted it to. She tried not to let the feeling that this perfect moment with Easy had just been ruined settle into her consciousness. Too late. She tried to steady her voice so it wasn't so shaky. 'So I noticed you've been flirting with Jenny . . .'

Easy backed away from her slightly. 'Noticed? What do you mean?'

'Well, you wrote all over her arm.'

He licked his lips. 'Oh.'

'So? Is it going okay?'

'I guess.'

'Have any teachers seen you, you know, flirting?'

'Um, just Mrs Silver, I guess . . .' Easy stood up and scratched his jaw.

Not good enough. It didn't matter if Mrs Silver had seen them – she wasn't friends with Ms Emory. 'Maybe you guys could flirt near the orchestra practice rooms?' Ms Emory conducted Waverly's orchestra, the Fermatas, on Sundays, Tuesdays, and Thursdays.

A long silence followed. Callie could hear the tree branches scrape against the windows.

Finally, Easy spoke. 'All you care about is whether or not you get in trouble, don't you?'

'No!' she squeaked. 'Of course not! I just—'

He held up his hand. 'This isn't right. It wasn't Jenny's fault. I don't think we should drag her into this, and I don't think she should have to take the fall for you.'

'What are you saying?' Callie demanded. 'You don't care if I get kicked out?' She felt tears spring to her eyes and quickly jammed her finger into her mouth. She bit hard, nearly drawing blood.

'No, of course I care, but—'

Callie shook her head. She could feel her pulse in her neck. 'No. You obviously don't. If you cared, you'd do whatever it took to keep me here.'

'Well, why would I want to keep you here if all you do is manipulate me?' Easy retorted loudly, his voice echoing through the silent library.

Callie's mouth dropped open. 'Excuse me?'

'You heard what I said,' he whispered fiercely.

'Take that back.'

Easy sighed. 'Callie . . . ' He trailed off, looking at her like he had no idea what to do with her.

She wasn't sure what possessed her to say what she said next, but she said it anyway: 'You know, Brandon would do this for me.'

'Brandon?' Easy asked. 'Brandon . . . Buchanan?' he scoffed.

Callie snapped back. 'Yeah, Brandon! At least Brandon—'

'At least he what?'

Paid attention to me, Callie thought. *At least I knew where I stood.* She swallowed hard and turned toward the window. Right outside, two owls huddled together on a tree branch. They looked like they were kissing.

Easy paced around the room. 'So, what, you want to break up with me to go out with Brandon again?'

Callie gasped. 'I didn't say that! Do you want to break up?' Her heart began to really pound. Was this it? All of a sudden she felt woozy and nauseated, as if she were about to fall off an endless cliff and was scrambling to hold on to its rocky side.

'Just stop manipulating me,' Easy blurted out sternly. 'If you think Brandon – who, by the way, is so gay – would do this for you, maybe you should be going out with him after all.'

'At least he loved me!' she pleaded. 'At least Brandon wanted to have sex!'

Her words hung in the air for a moment. Easy's lips parted, as if he were about to say something. But then a knock sounded at the heavy oak door. They both froze.

'Hello?' called a low voice. It was Mr Haim, the nasal-voiced, grumpy general librarian. 'Problem in there?'

Callie glared at Easy, baring her teeth before answering sweetly, 'We're just studying!'

'You have to keep it down,' Mr Haim whispered. He opened the door and stuck his Brillo-haired head through the crack. 'We don't tolerate noise in this room.'

'Whatever,' Easy yelled, flipping his middle finger up

in the air and straightening his shirt. 'I'm out of here.' He brushed by Mr Haim without even looking back at Callie to say goodbye.

'This is a place of peaceful research,' Mr Haim recited, tightening his Waverly tie almost to the point of asphyxiation. 'We don't tolerate yelling.'

'I said I was sorry!' Callie screamed.

'You're still yelling.'

She rolled her eyes. What the *hell* had just happened? She clomped down the marble stairs that led into the main lobby of the library. Out a tall, narrow window, she saw the same cuddling owls, this time on a lower tree branch. She stopped and knocked on the pane, causing the owls to ruffle their feathers and flutter to separate trees.

'Get a room!' she yelled.

OwlNet

To: Undisclosed list
From: CelineColista@waverly.edu
Time: Friday, September 6, 9:02 P.M.
Subject: TOP SECRET

Dumbarton pre–Black Saturday Party:

Welcome to Agrabah, City of Mystery and Enchantment.

GIRLS ONLY!

TEN MINUTES!

MOVE YOUR ASS!

25

A WAVERLY OWL MUST NEVER ANSWER HER ROOMMATE'S CELL PHONE WHILE DRUNK.

Callie was wearing the new fringed Kelly green Prada dress she'd bought at Pimpernel's, a multicolored Pucci headscarf, and four-inch-high silver Manolos. Her long strawberry-blond hair was swept up into a sexy, Asian-inspired bun, and she'd put thick kohl eyeliner around her eyes. She knew the other girls would be jealous, but that was the point. Sometimes it was more fun to dress up when there *weren't* boys around.

The pre-Black Saturday party was a tradition for Dumbarton girls. It was incredibly cool because there was a select guest list and there was always a wild theme. Benny Cunningham and Celine Colista had skipped out of field hockey practice early to convert the top-level common room into an Arabian Nights wonderland. They'd closed the giant bay window curtains so the whole room was shadowy and mysterious. Then they added twinkling lights, candles, pillows, incense, Grey Goose vodka, mini joints, pictures of elephants and multiarmed gods on the wall, and carefully placed *Kama Sutras*, which everybody knew were ancient sex manuals from India, and some bizarre, sexy Bhangra music Benny had gotten FedExed from Amazon.com the night before. The room was all set up for a wild orgy, except for the fact that there were no boys.

Callie had arrived early and was drinking quickly and steadily, trying to put the whole Easy-in-the-rare-book-room nightmare out of her mind. She refilled her drink and headed toward the little window seat in the corner and suddenly collided with Brett, who had just arrived.

'Oh!' They eyed one another intensely. Brett still had on what she'd worn to class, boring maroon Katayone Adeli trousers and a white Calvin Klein button-down. *Hello*? It was totally against the rules to wear that kind of thing to the pre-Black Saturday party! 'So, how's Jeremiah?' Callie asked.

'Jeremiah?' Brett gave her a blank look.

'Your boyfriend?'

'Oh, yeah.'

'What, is he not your boyfriend anymore?'

'No, he . . .' Brett was really squirming. Callie wondered if Sage was wrong – maybe instead of Brett liking a senior boy, she and Jeremiah had had really bad sex. Or, maybe really *good* sex. Earth to Brett, not dishing on any kind of sex to your so-called best friend was so not okay.

Then Brett narrowed her eyes keenly at Callie. 'And how's Easy?'

'Fine.'

They sat awkwardly on the window seat, looking past each other, sipping from their liquor-filled Waverly mugs. Last year, Callie, Brett, and Tinsley had sat around the pre-Black Saturday party in this very same common room, talking about their boyfriends and taking turns refilling one another's cups. What a difference a year made.

Callie tossed her hair behind her shoulder, eyeing her friend. Was it possible Brett was just waiting for her to broach the Tinsley subject so that Brett could apologize for getting Tinsley kicked out? One thing that Brett had never been good at was making herself vulnerable. 'I bet Tinsley would've been really into this party.'

Brett flinched, then murmured, 'Yeah, she would've.'

'It's too bad she's not here,' Callie continued quietly. *Okay, now we're getting somewhere.*

Brett straightened up. 'Yes, it is too bad she isn't here, isn't it?'

Wait, huh? That wasn't what Callie had been expecting Brett to say. Where was the *I'm so sorry, let me tell you what really happened or at least a Let's forget all of this ever happened and go get drunk in our room and catch up?* Instead, the two girls stared at each other like two dogs sniffing one another out, trying to figure out whether they wanted to bark or not. Suddenly, a crazy Hindi techno song blared through the speakers. The rest of the guests had arrived, and the room was jammed with bizarrely dressed girls who stank of Dior Poison.

'Conga line!' Benny squealed. She wore a lavender towel turban on her head and a kaleidoscopic Pucci scarf around her midriff. Sage grabbed her waist and giggled, a large Waverly crest flag wound around her body, sari style. They passed Callie and Brett and giggled.

'Come on, ladies!' Celine squealed. 'Stop with those pissy faces!'

Brett, who normally would have danced *Swan Lake* wearing a rabbit-fur muff if it meant being the life of the party, stood up, brushed off her lap, and shrugged. 'I'm out.' Then she turned and strode out of the room.

Callie wound a thick piece of Kelly green fringe around her middle finger and watched her go. Something buzzed next to her. It was Brett's tiny Nokia. The caller ID said Brianna Messerschmidt. Callie looked up and started to call for Brett but then stopped. Last year, she always used to answer Brett's phone when she left it somewhere. Were things so different this year she couldn't take the call? She snapped the phone open.

'Hey, it's Callie!'

'Where *are* you?' cried Bree in a sexy, husky smoker's voice. 'Spice Market? It sounds fabulous!'

Callie sank back down into the lounge chair. 'Nope. Just a dorm party.'

'I've *got* to do a shoot at your school sometime.'

'That would be awesome.' Callie wished Bree would give

some of her enthusiasm to her nasty younger sister. 'Should I find Brett?'

'Nah, tell her to call me. I'm home visiting our parents in Jersey this weekend.'

Jersey? As in New Jersey? She'd always thought Brett was from East Hampton . . .

'But listen, Callie? That teacher my sister's been hanging around? Like going to dinner with and stuff?'

'Uh—' Callie practically choked on a huge sip of punch. *What?*

'Eric Dalton? She told you about this, right?'

'Um, of course.' Callie's whole body began to sweat. She'd only eaten a couple of spoonfuls of Stonyfield vanilla yogurt this morning. A mug of vodka punch, and she was drunk. Her head spun: Brett was keeping more than a few secrets from her, all right.

Bree took a deep breath on the other end. 'So listen. When I was a senior at Columbia, a friend of mine was sort of Eric Dalton's girlfriend. And she told me he really gets around. You know what I'm saying?'

''Course,' Callie replied automatically. Maybe Brett wasn't acting spacey because she'd slept with Jeremiah. Maybe she was out of it because she'd slept with Eric Dalton. Callie fumbled in her bag for her cigarettes. How dare Brett not tell her this major news! *Hello*, were they just *complete* strangers now?

'But how funny,' Bree continued, snorting with laughter. 'Maybe they'll get married at St Patrick's! My sister will be a Dalton!'

Forgetting her buzz, Callie took another huge gulp of her drink. 'Don't you think she's a little young for him?'

'Oh, of course. I would rather he stay fifty feet away from her at all times, but Brett's got a good head on her shoulders. Anyway, just be sure to pass on the message? And tell her to call me. Ciao.'

'Um, okay. Ciao.'

Callie stared at the phone's tiny LED window for a long time, mashing her lips together. Finally, she looked up. The conga line was still snaking around the room.

Fuck it. Vodka punch burning in her stomach, she let out a whoop, grabbed Alison Quentin, who was wearing a vintage couture Alexander McQueen dress and tiny little olive leaves in her hair, and followed the line of gorgeous, drunk, dancing girls out into the hall.

26

A WAVERLY OWL SHOULD ALWAYS RESIST ADVANCES FROM HIS DRUNK EX-GIRLFRIEND.

B randon was cutting across Dumbarton's sprawling lawn toward Richards when he saw a girl in a flapper-style green dress smoking a cigarette and kicking her legs in the air like a Rockette.

'Hey, sweetie!' she called. 'Come dance with me.'

Brandon walked over and squinted in the light. It was Callie. Was she trashed? 'Hey,' he called out.

As soon as he got closer, she lunged at him and buried her face in his neck.

She smelled of fruit punch and cigarettes and that fresh chamomile shampoo she always used. Brandon felt a shudder run through him. Smelling Callie's hair conjured up memories of last year. They'd undressed each other under a quilt in the common room late one night and spelled out sexy messages on each other's bare stomachs. She looked up at him with giant, watery eyes.

'Brandon. *Hiiiii.*'

That's when he got a whiff of her breath. 'Whoa.' She was *definitely* trashed. 'You drink the whole bottle yourself?'

Callie righted herself and smiled. 'I'm cool,' she cooed. 'Want some of my cigarette?'

'No, thanks.'

Callie shrugged and stuck it back in her mouth. 'So listen,' she slurred, running her long, manicured fingernails up and down his bare arm. 'Why were you so mean to me after bio class yesterday?'

In the porch light, Brandon could see little goosebumps on her bare, creamy legs. 'About Easy and Jenny? I was telling the truth.'

'No, you weren't,' she teased, tipsily touching his nose. 'Nobody's stealing anybody away from me. I'm behind the whole thing.'

Brandon scowled. 'No, Callie. Jenny *likes* him. They like each other.'

Callie giggled. 'That's because I told them to like each other.'

'Huh?'

'I told them to like each other.' She covered her mouth and giggled. 'Oops. That was supposed to be a secret.'

Brandon shook his head. 'But Jenny *does* like him. And he likes her.'

'That's what they'd like you to believe!' Callie yelled, and then covered her mouth. 'Get it?' she slurred more quietly and broke into a goofy grin. 'They're faking it so that I won't get in trouble for having Easy in my room!'

Brandon stood back and thought for a moment. Yesterday in the quad, Jenny had sounded way too genuine to be faking it. 'And they both went along with this?'

'Yeah.'

'Jenny too?'

'Sure. Jenny's cool.' Callie flicked the ash off her cigarette, but she was so drunk that it landed right on her big toe, blackening it.

Brandon shook his head. He looked at Callie, who, though hammered, looked as if she'd been secretly crying in the girls' bathroom for hours. He wanted to cradle her and rock her to sleep.

'I mean, *you'd* flirt with another girl if I asked you to, wouldn't you?' she asked, slurring her words.

'Uh . . . no?' Brandon stuck his hands in his pockets.

She looked down, frustrated. 'You wouldn't?'

Brandon lowered his eyes. 'If I were going out with you, I wouldn't even look at another girl.'

'Oh, Brandon,' she sighed. 'You're so cheesy.'

Funny. He thought girls *liked* romance.

She snapped her fingers, brightening. 'Hey! So what do you think about Brett sleeping with that Mr Dalton guy?'

'What? I hadn't heard that.'

Callie threw both her hands over her mouth and

then slowly removed them. 'Maybe I shouldn't have said that . . .' She bit her lip. 'Oops.'

'It's, like, public news?' Brandon hadn't really met Mr Dalton except at chapel the first day, but it seemed highly sleazy for a teacher to hit on a student, let alone sleep with one.

'I don't know.' She looked down at the grass. 'I didn't know, but Brett doesn't tell me anything anymore, so . . .' She trailed off.

Brandon wasn't sure, but it seemed like she was about to burst into tears.

'Hey . . .' He reached his hand out to her. 'You okay?'

Suddenly, Callie threw her cigarette into the grass, grabbed Brandon, and gave him a huge, wet kiss on the mouth. At first he resisted, but after tasting her DuWop mint lip gloss, he couldn't help but melt into her. The kiss felt so good. Warm, soft, and sweet, just like a year ago. He thought of football games wrapped under blankets, the wobbly Metro-North train to the city where she'd fallen asleep in his lap, and playing footsie at formal dinner.

But then he pushed her away. He wanted this – he'd dreamed so many times of kissing Callie again – but this, right now, was wrong. All wrong.

'What's the matter?' Callie shrieked drunkenly, staggering backwards.

'You're really wasted.' Brandon shook his head. 'We shouldn't do this . . . now.'

'I'll tell you a secret,' she whispered, leaning into him. 'Easy and I had a big fight. I think we might be oooooover.'

He paused for a long time. Again, he'd waited forever to hear those words. But no, not now. Not like this. Brandon knew he was cheesy, but that was because he was a romantic. And fooling around with the girl he loved while she was shitfaced and on the rebound was totally fucking dumb. 'That's . . . whatever.' He pulled away from her.

'Come *on*,' Callie called. 'Don't you want to have sex with me?'

'You're drunk. You should sleep this off.'

And just like that, he wiped his mouth off and walked away.

OwlNet　　　　　Instant Message Inbox

BennyCunningham:　Hey. Did u send her the cheer words yet?

CallieVernon:　Not yet.

BennyCunningham:　Well, do it!

CallieVernon:　I will. Hey, what cheer are the rest of us doing?

BennyCunningham:　I dunno. What about 'Be Aggressive'?

CallieVernon:　K.

BennyCunningham:　Don't forget to send her the cheer, unless you want nippleless bras!

OwlNet   Instant Message Inbox

To: JenniferHumphrey@waverly.edu
From: CallieVernon@waverly.edu
Date: Saturday, September 7, 10:05 A.M.
Subject: Cheer

Hey Jenny,

You missed a great party last night. How was your new students' thing?

Anyway, Benny asked me to send you the words of the cheer. It involves some dancing – sexy! And you sing it to the tune of 'Sound Off'. I'm attaching a Word doc of the cheer lyrics here, and I'll show you the movements in the room, K?

– C

P.S. Did the KissKiss! beauty basket arrive today? Enjoy!

P.P.S. Any more thoughts about what you're going to say at DC? Let me know!

WAVERLY OWLS KNOW HOW — AND WHEN — TO BE AGGRESSIVE.

Everyone was hanging out on the vast green hockey field, which was surrounded by thick woods. The sun was directly above them, and the sky was a flawless blue, with a tiny bit of bite in the air. Parents, students, and alumni crowded the bleachers. The St Lucius girls paraded out to their side of the field. They were dressed in their purple and white sweaters and skirts, with matching purple shin guards. The St Lucius mascot, a giant black and white Canadian goose, followed behind them, flapping its wings menacingly at the bespectacled Waverly owl.

Brett picked some stray grass off the bottom of one of her Nike cleats and snorted at how stupid the owl looked. She couldn't help thinking of the Dorothy Parker quote,

'Men seldom make passes at girls who wear glasses.' An owl in glasses seemed like the nerdiest mascot ever.

Jenny sat next to her, tensely wrapping and unwrapping the duct tape around her hockey stick.

'So how was that party last night?' Jenny asked. 'I heard you guys come in last night really late . . .'

'That was Callie, not me,' Brett corrected her. 'I tried to slide in without you noticing. You didn't miss much, though. Except I lost my cell phone. Have you seen it?'

'No.' Jenny shrugged.

Brett gritted her teeth. Not having her cell phone – she was *always* losing it – meant she had no idea if Jeremiah or Eric had called. She wondered if Jeremiah was here in the crowd. She scanned the group of people across the field but didn't see a tall, cute boy with floppy red hair anywhere. She wondered how he'd taken her message the other night.

'So, I'm excited for the cheer.' Jenny grinned. 'It sounds like it's going to be really fun.'

Brett abruptly turned to her. 'You know it's a setup, right?' *Screw Callie.*

'A setup?' Jenny's eyes widened.

'Yeah, it's this—' Brett started, but just then Callie came up behind them and laid her hand on Jenny's shoulder. Brett turned away.

'Hey, girl,' Callie said sweetly to Jenny. 'You look so cute today. Is that my Stila lip gloss you're wearing?'

'Uh, no. It's mine. It's MAC.'

'It's so pretty.' Brett noticed Callie looked slightly green, probably from too much of that vile punch last night. Nice how she didn't even say hi to her. She was too busy kissing Jenny's ass.

'Benny came up to the group. 'We ready for the cheer?'

'Yeah,' Callie agreed. She looked nervously at Jenny. Jenny looked nervously at Brett. Brett shrugged. This was their shit to figure out.

'Let's go, then!' Benny squealed.

All the girls on the bench jumped up and began to bounce on the balls of their feet. They'd asked Devin Rausch, a senior whose dad was a famous record producer, to play drums and DJ. Callie gave him a nod. The needle crackled on an old Funkadelic record: he scratched it a few times, and then the backbeat wafted out of the speakers. The girls started to stomp their feet.

'Be. Aggressive. B-E aggressive . . .'

Brett, who stood at the back of the gang, mouthed the words. This was so dumb. She glanced over at Jenny, who launched into her part of the cheer.

'St Lucius girls think they're all that, but no one wants a girl that flat!'

Jenny heard her solo screechy voice and immediately covered her mouth. Unfortunately, she was also at the portion of the dance where she had to stick out her chest. She looked over and noticed that no one *else* had thrust their boobs out.

Her teammates snorted with laughter. Jenny froze, boobs still thrust out. So this was the setup. Ha, ha. So *not* funny.

Things began to move in slow motion: the laughing girls, stupid mean Heath Ferro slapping his thigh in the front row, the entire school staring at her gigantic boobs.

Then she realized something. She knew she could either feel like total shit and act like Old Jenny, who, mortified, would sit back down on the bench and never speak to anybody ever again. Or she could try and turn this situation into something interesting. After all, this might be her last weekend at Waverly. So before she could stop herself, Jenny strode up to the front of the team and started belting out the lyrics of the bogus cheer Callie had e-mailed her in her loudest voice.

'St Lucius girls think they're all that, but no one wants a girl that flat!' Jenny started, shoving out her double-Ds again. 'Waverly girls get all the boys! C'mon, people, make some noise!' She made a swishing motion with her hips.

'Our eyebrows are waxed and yours are bushy; our butts are cute and yours are cushy!' Then she hit herself hard on her adorable little round butt. The other girls' mouths dropped open. 'Our mascot's an owl and yours is a goose! We've got hooters and y'all are loose!' Again with the boob-thrusting.

'So c'mon, St Lucius, throw in the towel. Your ass is gonna get kicked by an owl!' Then Jenny, as she'd been instructed, ran crazily lengthwise down the field and did three cartwheels, as best she could, showing the crowd what-ever they hadn't already seen of her baby-blue boy shorts.

A dazed silence followed. Even though the words were totally ridiculous, every single Waverly and St Lucius boy – not to mention the fathers and male teachers – was gazing at her.

Then, across the field, Lance Van Brachel, one of

Waverly's star football players, started to clap. 'Yeah!' he screamed. 'Hell yeah!'

Another boy clapped slowly. Someone whistled. Then the whole other side of the field erupted in applause. Everyone began to go nuts.

Brett stared at Jenny, who was standing with her arms stretched out, staring dazedly at the crowd, a huge smile on her face. Jenny had just twisted Callie's manipulation, something even Tinsley had never managed to pull off. Jenny seemed so unafraid of people paying attention to her, and her curvy, tiny body looked great dancing. She had a good shouting voice, too – hoarse and kind of sexy.

Jenny looked at her adoring fans across the field. Wow, this was fun! Then she had a flash of inspiration.

'There is a boy who they call Pony! He's always acting gross and horny!' she yelled at the top of her lungs. 'He thinks he's got a lot down there, but he sure wears tiny underwear!'

The Waverly bleachers went wild. A bunch of boys covered their mouths and yelled a collective 'Oh!' in Heath's direction. Everyone was laughing. Jenny looked at Heath in the front row – his face was an angry red. *Gotcha*.

'Let's do it again!' Jenny launched back into the cheer, hardly noticing the other girls. They were all party poopers. If they didn't want to cheer with her, she didn't care. She felt free and crazy.

Brett was dumbfounded. Suddenly, she grinned, and ran up to join Jenny.

'St Lucius girls think they're all that, but no one wants

a girl that flat!' they screamed together. Jenny smiled and bumped her butt against Brett's hip. At the end of the cheer, Brett even did the skirt-lift. The boys across the field went crazy.

Then Celine joined in, too. Then Alison, then Benny. Then the rest of the girls. And finally, because it would look weird if she were the only field hockey player *not* cheering, Callie started shouting too.

28

A WAVERLY OWL SHOULD KNOW
THAT FUNNER ISN'T A WORD.

Buoyed by their cheer, the Waverly Owls beat the St Lucius Geese 6 to 3. As soon as the final period's buzzer sounded, Brett hustled to her dorm room. There, on her bed, was her cell phone. Had she left it on her bed all this time? On it were three unanswered calls – all from her sister – and one text message: *I'm in port. Come by if you want. – ED.*

She quickly pulled on her most flattering it's-getting-crisp-at-night-weight Joseph pants and slinkiest Diane von Furstenberg sleeveless silk top and zipped on her pointiest black patent leather boots. She sprinted down to the water-front.

Eric stood on the white sailboat's small deck wearing

khakis and a green long-sleeved polo. He was holding binoculars up to his eyes and was gazing at something in the trees. A fishing pole was propped against the boat's railing. When he heard her behind him, he turned around, the binoculars still pressed to his eyes. Brett instinctively covered her chest, as if they were x-ray glasses.

'No football game for you?' he asked, putting the binoculars down.

'Nah.'

'Isn't the football game the biggest part of the day?'

Yeah, except her ex-boyfriend happened to be the other team's star quarterback. Brett wasn't exactly sure if Jeremiah had even gotten the I-need-a-break message she'd left on his voice mail, but she kind of didn't care. 'I'm not really into football,' she replied coyly. 'May I have permission to board?'

He laughed. 'Yeah, sure.'

'So.' She ran her hands over the boat's chrome rails. 'Does this thing have a name?'

'Not yet. She's brand-new,' Eric answered, his piercing gray eyes on her. 'I was thinking about something from Hemingway.'

Brett's insides scrambled up. *Like maybe something from The Sun Also Rises?* she wanted to ask.

'What field hockey position do you play again?'

'Oh, center,' she responded, as if it didn't matter, even though she'd played field hockey since she was seven and had scored two of the six goals today.

He chuckled, then picked up the fishing pole.

'Why is that funny?'

'It's not. It's just, I can't imagine you in a field hockey outfit.'

'Have you tried? Imagining it, I mean.' Brett smiled coquettishly. She was being bold, even for her.

'Maybe.' Eric's eyes were on her. 'It's a pretty short kilt. You girls shorten them, don't you?'

'Of course not!' Brett lied. 'They're that short to begin with!'

She sat down on one of the captain's chairs and stared out at the glistening water. Waverly's chapel spire peeked up through the elegant, blue-green thicket, and the owls criss-crossed overhead, as if magnetically drawn to the yacht. Even the water smelled sexy.

'So, I wanted to thank you for the other night,' she finally ventured. 'The plane. Dinner. Seeing your family's house. It was really fun.'

Dalton removed the binoculars from around his neck. 'I'm glad.'

A cheer rose up from the football stadium in the distance, and the band started to play. Brett glanced over in its direction, wondering who had scored. Jeremiah was probably on the field right this second.

Brett looked over at Eric. Biting her lip, she stood up and took a tiny step in his direction. 'So, yeah, it was fun, but . . .'

'But what?' Eric paused.

Brett thought she detected something funny in his voice. She felt like she was standing on the edge of a cliff that overlooked the turquoise Caribbean Sea. It was either turn around and head back to the bungalow to drink a Red Stripe in the hammock or dive off the cliff. She took a huge gulp of air.

'Do you think that there was something maybe that could've been *funner*?' Brett asked, twisting her head to the side.

'*Funner* isn't a word.' Eric smirked. Water lapped at the side of the boat.

'Yeah, I know,' she whispered, lowering her eyes, feeling young and dumb. *Go back to the bungalow! Now!* Fighting her better judgment, she batted her eyelashes and stuck out her chest. She had no idea where she was getting these moves from. Jenny, maybe? She heard Eric breathe in sharply.

Fuck it. She was diving. She walked right up to where he stood, still fishing. He was a few inches taller than she was. His blondish hair fell messily over his eyes, and he had a tiny scratch on the side of his nose. He propped his fishing pole against the railing again.

'Maybe *this* could be . . . funner?' Then she leaned her entire body against his and kissed him. *Ahh, yes.*

His mouth felt amazing. Brett tried to restrain herself, but part of her wanted to devour him, like he was Beluga caviar. She kept kissing him, softly at first, willing his lips to part until finally his strong hands circled her waist and his lips melted around hers. He pulled her closer. Her mouth opened. Brett worried that she tasted like sweat from the game, but she didn't care. Nor did she care that they were in broad daylight, on Waverly's campus, on Black Saturday, and the whole school was only half a mile away.

She stopped kissing him and took a step back, smiling shyly.

Eric licked his lips. It looked like he was trying to hide a grin. 'Um, well. That's, uh, definitely . . .' He took her hand in his, and his eyes met hers. He chewed on his lower lip a little. 'So I think . . . I think I should go back to my office for a while.'

'Great. Let's go,' Brett replied, smiling. 'Now.'

Dalton steeled himself against the railing. 'I mean, I think I should go back to my office and I think *you* should go back to your football game,' he whispered, his hand brushing her ear.

Brett stepped away from him and looked frantically back in the direction of the stadium. Eric stepped off the yacht. He reached out for her and helped her onto the dock too.

'If I come to your office, you won't regret it.' She'd never said anything like that to anybody in her life.

'I realize that.' Eric sighed. 'Believe me. I most definitely realize that. But, um . . .' He looked down at his navy blue Docksider boat shoes. 'I think . . . I think I should go. But thank you.'

And with that, he stuck his thumb out, touched her on the chin, and turned, leaving Brett and her beautiful black pointy boots, standing on a stupid boat dock, alone.

29

WAVERLY OWLS NEVER TURN DOWN A GAME OF I NEVER — EVEN IF IT MEANS KISSING HEATH FERRO.

Brandon stood, gin and tonic in hand, talking to Benny Cunningham at the Black Saturday party, which was, surprise surprise, at Heath Ferro's country house in Woodstock, about an hour away from Waverly. He saw Jenny spill out of a Hummer with a group of field hockey girls. They were all dressed up in matching pumpkin-colored slouchy V-neck cashmere sweaters. Jenny's sweater showed off her beautiful porcelain skin and exposed some of her bare shoulders, and he could see a wide, cream-colored bra strap.

After the football game, Heath had handed Waverly's elite overnight off-campus passes and ushered everyone toward a fleet of black Hummer limos that he'd borrowed from his dad's Wall Street I-banking firm. Brandon had watched from a distance as Heath approached Jenny, who was flanked by gaggle of admirers, kissed her primly on the cheek, and handed her a pass. Even he had to give her props for the cheer.

The party took place on the house's massive back lawn. It was warm and still out, and Heath had had the gardener install a giant white tent and rows of twinkly Christmas lights. He'd also nabbed six giant sculptures from his parents' ever-growing collection of random gallery purchases to decorate the expansive tent. The sculptures were gigantic blooming lilies. Their lustrous folds reminded everyone not so subconsciously of sex. As if anyone needed another reminder of sex. After watching Jenny's chest, it was all anyone could think about.

Jenny spied Brandon and hurried over. 'Hey! Where'd you go after the game?' she exclaimed brightly.

'Just took off for here a little early, I guess,' he answered, then looked away fast. He still felt all messed up over this Callie-Easy-Jenny business.

'What's the matter?' she asked.

'Nothing.'

'Jenny, that cheer was totally fun.' Benny squeezed Jenny's hand. Benny's Mikimoto freshwater pearl earrings were so big they made her earlobes droop.

'Thanks!' Jenny cried.

'Brandon, did you see it?'

'I saw it.' It would have been hard not to see it. It had

been kind of slutty but kind of hot at the same time. And his brain had felt like it was going to explode, watching both Jenny and Callie stick out their chests and smack their butts at the same time. And of course he'd relished watching Heath shrivel in embarrassment when Jenny called him out on his small weenie.

Jenny eyed him carefully. 'Seriously, you all right?'

'Eh,' Brandon murmured.

'What's the matter?' she asked again. Benny shimmied away to hang around someone else. 'You can tell me.'

He mashed his lips together. He didn't know what he was feeling. Was he confused about Callie? Pissed at Jenny for being so into Easy? Annoyed to be back at school, period? Suddenly an alarmingly high-pitched voice pealed over the crowd.

'Jenny!' Brandon and Jenny's heads swiveled. Celine sat across the room, on a pristine white leather couch. Brett, dressed all in black, sat on the couch's arm. Callie stood on the other side, smoking through a thin silver cigarette holder. Brandon's heart started thudding. 'Jenny, c'mere!' Celine crowed.

Jenny looked back at Brandon. 'You sure you're all right?' she asked.

'*Jen-ny!*' Celine squealed again.

Jenny looked at him questioningly a few moments more, and Brandon realized he was kind of being a jackass. So Callie was screwing with his emotions. So Jenny didn't like him. So what? She was still sweet and caring. And right now, she seemed so *happy*. 'Seriously,' he ordered. 'Go.'

As Jenny skipped over to the girls' couch, a tall, cocksure senior girl named Chandler grabbed her arm. 'Cool cheer.'

'Thank you!'

Another blond girl standing next to Chandler who wore a slinky silver top and pegged pink and gray pinstriped pants, squinted at Jenny. 'Did you ever model? You look so familiar.'

'I think she looks like Tinsley,' Chandler added.

'Actually, I modeled for a Les Best ad? But it was only once.' Jenny beamed.

'No, that's it!' the girl cried. 'I love that ad. You look so cute in it, all crazy on the beach. Who was your stylist?'

'*Jenny!*' Celine called from the couch again.

'I gotta go,' Jenny explained to Chandler and the other girl. 'Nice meeting you!' As she was walking toward the couch again, it suddenly hit her. She didn't feel compelled to make up some crazy story about a seminaked fashion show or a debauched night out with the Raves. Nope. Jenny – not Old Jenny or New Jenny, but this Jenny – was good enough for these girls just as she was. *I love Waverly!* she thought, with a momentary shiver of pleasure. God, she just couldn't get kicked out. Not now!

She joined the others on the couch. Celine immediately handed her a Grey-Goose-and-Red-Bull Martini.

'So you're not pissed at us?' Celine asked. 'About the cheer?'

'Yeah.' Callie shook her head. 'I wanted to tell you . . .'

'Don't worry about it,' Jenny assured them. Even though

it had been kind of mean, she felt like she was a part of something now – a real, *exclusive* Waverly tradition. How awesome was that?

'That cheer was amazing, though,' Celine commented. She was sucking on a Dunhill Ultra Light and a pastel candy necklace at the same time.

Jenny moved over to Brett, who was sitting on the far end of the couch and looked like she'd been up for 96 hours. 'You disappeared after the game. You all right?'

'I don't know,' Brett replied mechanically.

'Is it—?' Jenny started.

Brett put her finger to her lips but nodded miserably. 'What happened?'

Brett shook her head. 'Can't talk about it,' she whispered between gulps.

'Okay.'

Callie grabbed Brett's arm. 'I saw Jeremiah when I was coming in. He's looking for you.'

Brett's eyes widened in fear. 'Did you tell him I was here?'

'Uh, yeah. Why, is there a reason I wouldn't?' she asked, obviously feigning obliviousness.

'Shit,' Brett muttered.

'What's the big deal? It's not like you're seeing anyone else, is it?'

Brett shook her head feverishly. 'You shouldn't have told him I was here.'

'Well, sorry! How was I supposed to know that?' Callie demanded. 'It's not like you tell me anything anymore.'

'You just . . . shouldn't have.'

The other girls' heads swiveled from Callie to Brett, as if watching the final match at Wimbledon. Jenny wondered if Callie knew about Brett and Mr Dalton. Callie put her cigarette out with the heel of her blue croc mule. 'So why don't you want to see Jeremiah, anyway?'

'I just . . . don't. Just because.'

'Is he not cool enough for you? Are *we* not cool enough for you?' Callie demanded, rolling her tongue against her cheek.

'Come on,' Brett retorted. 'I didn't say—'

'You looking for some *older* people to hang out with?' Jenny froze.

Brett scowled. 'What's that supposed to mean?'

Callie tilted her head. 'Did you find your cell phone?'

'Yeah.' Brett lit a cigarette. 'So?'

'So . . . nothing. I found it. Just making sure you got it.'

'Did you go through my messages?' Brett's voice rose sharply.

'No!' Callie sounded hurt. 'I wouldn't do that!'

'Like hell you wouldn't. Whatever. I have to get the fuck out of here.'

'What's she talking about?' Celine asked as Brett stormed away.

Callie stared fumingly at Brett's receding figure and didn't answer.

'Sounds like she's having boy problems – she didn't even want to see Jeremiah!' Celine added. 'And he's so hot!'

'Oh, it's not Jeremiah she's having the problems with,' Callie whispered. 'It's, you know – *Mr Dalton*.'

Jenny's mouth dropped open. Oh. My. God. Some friend Callie was.

'Dalton?' Celine echoed. The girls stared at her in stunned silence.

'Totally. They're really—' Callie began smugly, but she was interrupted by Heath Ferro. He wore a fake wooden Viking helmet, à la Flava Flav, on his head and had taken his shirt off to reveal a temporary Celtic symbol tattoo on his chest.

'Hey, girls.' He slung his arms around Jenny and Callie. *I guess he likes me again*, Jenny thought wryly. Not that she cared. 'I'm horny.' He pointed to the horns.

Celine giggled. 'Ew!'

''Course you are, Pony,' cried Benny, who'd come up behind them.

'That's right. So you want to play I Never?' Heath grabbed a bottle of Cuervo from a nearby table.

'Definitely,' Callie agreed quickly, wrenching her eyes away from Brett, who'd paused at the tent's door, her whole body quivering.

'Okay, but new rules: if you've never done it you have to take a shot and kiss someone,' Heath announced, fondling one of the horns on his helmet.

'You're unbelievable.' Benny laughed.

'Fine,' Callie sighed. 'Just no tongue.'

Jenny, Heath, Sage, Teague Williams, and Benny arranged themselves on the dewy grass just outside the tent.

The air was cool and wet, but Jenny felt warm from her belly out. Her Red Bull Martini was making her feel a little weird.

'Who wants to go first?' Heath asked, taking a long chug of Heineken.

'I will.' Jenny shot her hand up. She poured out shots into small plastic cups. 'Okay. So. Um . . . I've never made out in a field.'

Callie, Celine, and Benny all shrugged. Jenny, Heath, and Teague each did a shot.

'C'mere, Jenny,' Heath beckoned, crawling across the circle toward her. 'Let's see if we can remember how to do this.'

Ew, ew, ew. Jenny tipsily pecked Heath's mouth and then smacked him playfully in the stomach.

'Jeepers!' she squealed. And instead of laughing at her, everyone cheered and did another shot, just for fun.

30

NOT ALL WAVERLY OWLS NEED GLASSES.

Easy inhaled deeply on the joint and handed it to Alan St Girard. They were sitting in a little alcove that separated them from the rest of the tent with those door beads that a grandmother might have in her pool house. 'This party's lame,' Easy managed to grumble, while trying to hold the pot smoke in his lungs.

'Aren't they always, though?' Alan replied.

They talked for a few minutes about which party had been the best, and decided that it was the one Tinsley Carmichael had thrown at her parents' huge log cabin in Alaska a year and a half ago. It had been over spring break, and most kids had been with their parents in Park City or Monte Carlo, so not that many of them had gone to Alaska. The house was on the edge of an ice lake, next to a giant, purple mountain. They'd all drunk so much red wine, they'd been completely uninhibited. It was before Easy and Callie got together, and he'd coaxed Tinsley into getting naked with him and sitting in her outdoor birch hot tub, where they'd talked all night. It had been the kind of party where everything is serene and perfect – nobody had gotten mad at anybody, and everybody had stayed on that fun, wild side of drunk without crossing over and vomiting all over the teak floors.

The beads parted, and Brett burst through. She was wearing all black and looked craggy and grumpy, like that wicked old witch with the apple in *Snow White*. 'What's up?' Easy asked, as she plopped down next to him.

'Can I hide out in here with you?' She took the joint, which had burned down to a little knobby roach. She took a long drag on it and blew the smoke out her nose.

'Sure.'

'You guys make no sense,' she finally said after a long pause, running her hands through her insanely red hair.

'What, me and Alan?'

'No.' Brett turned to Easy, and Easy remembered why he liked her so much. She had a wide-jawed, wide-eyed, beautiful face, a little like Mandy Moore's. 'I meant . . . why is it that when you guys want something, and when you get it, when we *give* it to you, you freak out?'

Alan took a hit and leaned back, running his hand along

his very short brown crew cut. 'That's way too deep for me, man.'

Brett pulled out her cigarettes and lit one. 'Never mind,' she scoffed, standing up again. She squinted at Easy. 'Are you still with Callie?'

'I don't know.'

She smirked. 'That's what I thought. I'm outta here. Have a good party, boys.'

'She's so strange,' Alan muttered. 'You know what I just heard? I heard she's fucking one of the teachers. That new guy.'

'Brett?' Easy asked, looking after her. 'Nah.'

'I don't know, man. Look at her. She's a mess.'

Easy grunted and rolled one of the beige marble door beads between his fingers. His pot-addled brain tried to process what had gone down with Callie. Were they still together or not?

He stood up and parted the beads with his hand, feeling totally messed up. He expected love to feel like something stupendous, maybe a little painful. Like the sore, used-up way his back and legs felt after riding Credo all day. Or the feeling he got when he was in Paris, standing on the Seine, watching people walk by, and suddenly realized he was *right there* in the moment and not stuck somewhere in the past or the future. But he wasn't sure if he felt that way about Callie. Where was she, anyway?

And that's when he saw them.

Heath Ferro kissing Callie all over her face. She'd pulled down Heath's jeans so low that they'd slid below his hips.

He could see a strip of his ass. As usual, Heath was going commando.

Easy turned into the alcove again. Well, there was his answer.

31

A WAVERLY OWL KNOWS THAT SOMETIMES IT'S A GOOD IDEA TO SIT IN THE SHADOWS.

'I feel all loose and wiggly.' Jenny shook her arms around. She'd moved to the surprisingly quiet lawn behind the tent. There was a tiny little Japanese rock garden, a mossy stone bench, and a jade-tile-lined pond. A giant orange goldfish swam slowly in the pond's circle. After a few rounds of I Never, Brandon had tapped her on the shoulder and asked her if she wanted to get some air.

'You were looking a little green back there,' Brandon said.

'I'm all right. But thanks for getting me out of that. It was getting a little strange.' She wasn't really keen on seeing Heath Ferro's butt crack, which kept making major appearances.

'No problem.'

'How come you didn't play with us? You got something against kissing games?'

'I . . .' He hesitated. 'It's complicated.'

Jenny rolled her head around on her neck. 'Okay,' she replied. She was happy that Brandon felt okay just sitting her with her quietly, not explaining anything. Friends sat quietly together, after all, and even though she was having a blast at this party, something in it seemed empty now that she was drunk. How many of these kids did she actually connect with? Brandon was a real friend, and they could be honest with each other. She leaned her head on his shoulder and stared at their reflection in the pond.

'You never told me you went out with Callie last year.' She glanced at him.

He looked down. 'Yeah.'

'Is that why you hate Easy so much?'

He nodded.

'Well. That makes sense.'

'It's so messed up, though,' Brandon began slowly. 'I still really like her. I tried to not like her but . . . I can't help it.'

'I totally understand,' she said, thinking of Easy.

Another reflection appeared in the pond. It was of a messy-haired, irresistibly handsome boy who, despite being at a party, still had paint smudges on his neck. Jenny drew in her breath. It was as if she had conjured Easy up by thinking about him.

Or maybe she was just a little tipsy.

'Hey.' He greeted her softly.

Jenny squinted. He wore a black faded NASHVILLE MUSIC FESTIVAL T-shirt and grubby, paint-stained jeans. His thick, glossy, almost-black hair, badly in need of cutting, curled at the back of his neck.

Brandon creased his face in frustration, then squeezed her hand. 'I should be going,' he announced. He leaned over and whispered in her ear, 'Good luck.'

Brandon brushed past Easy without saying hello, then slowly strode away. Easy sat down next to Jenny. 'What are you doing out here? There's all sorts of crazy shit going on in this place.'

'Yeah, I was part of the crazy shit, but I decided to come out and look at the pond.'

'Pretty,' Easy murmured.

'It is, isn't it?'

'I mean you, not the pond,' he whispered.

Jenny's words got stuck in her throat. She was too, too drunk. But suddenly she felt too, too sober. Easy lit a cigarette and smoked it silently, letting a thin stream of gray smoke drift over the gardens and make a halo over the origami trees.

'I saw your cheer at the game today.' Easy broke the silence. 'That was . . . something.'

'Oh,' she managed to utter, looking down, embarrassed. The drunker Jenny had gotten, the more she had wondered if she really belonged here. So she'd turned the cheer around today, but what if she couldn't keep up that kind of quick thinking all the time? She kept trying not to think about it, but heavy thoughts about the Disciplinary Committee hearing kept sneaking up on her. Sure, she was popular tonight, but what did that matter if she was kicked out of Waverly come Monday? Then again, she could tell on Callie, but everyone would definitely hate her if she got Callie kicked out. There was no way to win.

'Where'd you learn that?'

'Actually . . . it's too weird to explain.'

'Huh,' Easy responded. 'So, you know how I told you about those owls in that note?'

'Yeah.' Jenny was looking at his profile out of the corner of her eye. The night was getting colder, and she could see dew forming on the grass around them. She wondered what time it was.

'Did you think that was totally stupid?'

Jenny crossed her legs. 'What? No. Why?'

'Because . . . I told you that I thought they talked.'

'No. Actually, I thought it was really sweet.'

'You did?' He smiled shyly at the ground.

'Yeah.' She smiled too, looking at him now.

Easy slid slightly closer to her. 'Why?'

Jenny thought about why. *Because you're hot? Because you're beautiful? Because I can't stop thinking about how perfect you are for me?*

Jenny sat back. 'Easy? Are you flirting with me because Callie told you to?'

He took a drag off his cigarette. 'I was going to ask you the same thing.'

'Oh,' she said, confused. She stared at her reflection in the pond. 'Well, are you?'

'No,' he finally answered. Jenny noticed that his hand was trembling. 'Are you?'

'No,' Jenny replied quickly. 'I'm definitely not.'

'What are you going to do about DC?' he asked after a few seconds, stubbing his cigarette out on a rock. 'Are you going to say it was Callie's fault?'

'I still haven't decided.' Jenny felt her face squinch up. She didn't want to ruin Callie's life, but she also didn't want to get kicked out of Waverly. What if she walked out of DC and never saw Easy again?

'Look,' Easy sighed. 'I don't think any of this is right, and I don't think you should be in trouble. And besides, I'm not even together with Callie anymore.'

Jenny held her breath.

'It's weird that she's manipulating us, you know?'

She nodded imperceptibly.

'And more than that . . . things don't feel right,' he whispered, as if he were talking to himself.

'What do you mean?' Jenny asked, willing him to meet her gaze and then, maybe . . . her lips.

'Well . . .' Easy leaned back in the grass and stared up at the sky. Jenny remembered how he'd pointed out the Seven Sisters on their ceiling and wondered where that constellation was tonight. 'You know how those De Beers diamond commercials show love as like this . . . this really sparkly, crazy thing?'

'Okay,' Jenny said, lying down on her back as well.

'Well, I want that,' Easy explained, talking straight ahead. 'I don't have that now, but I want it. Not in a stupid way, but I want all of that.'

Jenny's insides shimmered. She understood what he meant completely. And as they stared up at the sky, the stars above them twinkled, shiny and sparkly. Kind of like diamonds.

OwlNet

To: 'partygoers' (27 members on list)
From: HeathFerro@waverly.edu
Date: Sunday, September 8, 11:40 A.M.
Subject: Awesome, awesome, awesome

Guys. The Black Saturday party was white-hot. Some interesting numbers:

6: Number of girls I made out with last night. (That's the number I can remember, anyway.)

11: Bottles of Cuervo we went through. Hells yeah!

1: Weirdly well-groomed guy standing on the sidelines of the I Never game, looking longingly at a certain blond goddess from Atlanta.

2: Left-behind pairs of girls' shoes. One pair of Manolos, one pair of Tod's. Who got so messed up she went home barefoot?

2: People sitting by my goldfish pond, looking longingly into each other's eyes. But I'm not gonna tell you who. That's only for my goldfish, Stanley, to know for sure.

Later, party people,

Heath

P.S. Can't wait for the next blowout.

P.P.S. It's only three weeks away. Rest up!

32

PLAYING A SPORT IS A HEALTHY WAY FOR
WAVERLY OWLS TO DEAL WITH THEIR
AGGRESSION.

The Waverly sports staff was so evil that they made everyone go to sports practice on Blacker Sunday (called that for obvious reasons). Everyone hit the field with stale-Martini breath, eye shadow still smeared on their upper lids, and pink tongues, courtesy of two big swigs of Pepto to calm their gurgling stomachs.

Callie sat on the hockey bench with her head between her legs. She had a hickey on her neck, and she was certain it wasn't from Easy. She'd tried to cover it with her Joey New York concealer stick, but the big purple welt was still there. Really, she felt too shitty to care. She wanted to curl back up under her double-thick cashmere blanket and suck her thumb. She eyed Jenny and Brett sitting on the grass, stretching, looking as if they hadn't had a sip of alcohol last night. Since when were they such good friends?

Mrs Smail blew her whistle and called the girls up to scrimmage. Of all things to do at a post-Black Saturday party practice, they were actually going to *play*? Why couldn't everyone do a couple of laps and go back to bed?

'Callie Vernon, Brett Messerschmidt, you'll play centers,' Mrs Smail instructed.

A collective gasp rose up from the bench. Everyone's heads swiveled back and forth, from Callie's blond ponytail to Brett's fire-red bob. Callie heaved herself up from the bench, feeling bloated and disgusting. She watched Brett storm off to the middle of the field. Frustration welled up inside of her again. How *dare* Brett not tell her about Mr Dalton!

As soon as Mrs Smail dropped the small silver ball, Brett whacked it, following through so roughly she hit Callie's left shin guard.

Callie backed up in pain and anger. She tore after Brett, who was now a few steps ahead of her, dribbling the ball. The sod was mushy under her feet, and her black and white Nike cleats dug fiercely into the ground. Brett's skirt rose so that you could see the bottom of her STX maroon bloomers and her skinny butt. Callie caught up to her and stuck her stick in between Brett and the ball. Then Brett's hands twisted and she whacked the ball with the rounded side of her hockey stick, sending it careening away from Callie, toward one of the midfielders on Brett's team.

'Foul!' Callie screamed, stopping in her tracks. 'Mrs Smail! That was a foul!'

'I didn't see it,' Mrs Smail responded. 'Keep playing.' She gestured to the other girls, who had taken the ball and swept it down toward one of the goals.

'Jesus Christ!' Callie threw her stick to the ground in disgust. 'She hit the ball with the wrong side of the stick!'

'Whatever,' Mrs Smail said. 'It's only practice, and I didn't see it.'

Callie turned to Brett, eyes narrowed. 'They don't teach field hockey in New Jersey, do they?'

Callie watched as Brett's milky-white skin turned whiter.

'Go to hell,' Brett finally muttered.

'Ooh, the big comeback from class prefect, Brett Messerschmidt. I thought you had great debate skills! I thought you could talk your way out of anything!'

'Girls,' Mrs Smail warned. 'Play. Brett, your team just scored a goal.'

Brett stepped around Mrs Smail to face Callie. 'What is it, Callie? What's the huge thing you have against me? If anything, I'm the one who should be angry at you – not the other way around!'

'Oh, yeah? Why's that?'

'Because you're a manipulative bitch, that's why!' Brett screamed.

The other players gasped. Mrs Smail tried to step between them, but Callie shot her a look of warning that said, *Stay away*. Mrs Smail turned and began walking briskly toward the field house.

Callie turned to Brett. 'You take that back. I'm not manipulative.'

Brett barked out a laugh. 'No? So what's this whole Jenny-and-Easy thing about? How is that not manipulation?' She shot a look over at Jenny, who was standing perfectly still, stick poised, watching them from her midfield position.

Callie glanced at Jenny too. Great. Just great. A comment like that wouldn't help sway Jenny to stick up for her at DC. She glowered at Brett. 'You don't know anything.'

'I don't have to know anything,' Brett shot back. 'I know you and how you operate. From what you did to Tinsley.'

'Tinsley?!?' Callie's mouth dropped open.

'That's right.' Brett's voice was hushed. She stepped closer to her former friend, so close that their noses were almost touching. 'Why don't you just come clean? You set Tinsley up to take the rap. You made it so you wouldn't get in any trouble.'

Oh, this was something. '*I* set it up? Who's to say *you* didn't set it up?' Callie yelled. Tears sprang to her eyes. 'I didn't even *talk* to Tinsley before she left! I was called into DC, I left, and she was already gone!'

'Oh, yeah. That's a good one—'

'Why would I set Tinsley up? We were friends!'

Brett stepped back and glared at Callie confusedly. They both stared at each other for a few long seconds before Brett's shoulders relaxed a bit. 'You're serious, aren't you?'

Callie nodded fiercely.

'And you think that *I* got Tinsley in trouble?'

'Well *I* didn't, so *you* must have,' Callie explained, but Brett could hear her resolve weakening.

'I didn't have a chance to talk to Tinsley, either. She was gone before I could.'

Callie looked down. 'Really?'

'Yes.'

The other players held their breath.

'I don't get it,' Brett surmised. 'Tinsley just . . . took the blame for us, on her own?'

'I guess. But why would she do that?'

'No clue.'

Callie began to laugh. 'That's really fucked up.'

Brett slowly began to giggle too. 'God, I totally thought you did it.'

'And I thought *you* did it!'

'*I* thought you were going to transfer rooms on me, just to avoid having to talk about Tinsley!'

Behind them, Mrs Smail ran up with Mr Steinberg, the boy's soccer coach, in tow. When she saw Callie and Brett laughing and then hugging, she stopped short in confusion.

'I swear they were ready to kill each other.'

'Girls,' Mr Steinberg sighed hopelessly, shaking his head.

33

A WAVERLY OWL SHOULD BE CAREFUL
NOT TO GET BUSTED.

Mrs Smail ran her fingers through her short honey-blond hair. 'You know, why doesn't everyone just hit the showers,' she suggested after a moment. *Finally.*

Brett felt like she'd just run a marathon, which was always how she felt after vigorously fighting with somebody. She walked slowly back to the bleachers with Callie, neither of them speaking. But it was a comfortable silence, not a tense one. She threw her shin guards in her Hervé Chapelier *cabas* gray nylon bag and noticed her cell phone buzzing. She had a text message: *Come meet me on my boat when you can. We need to talk. – Eric.*

She put her head in her hands. That single lingering

kiss. His soft lips. The way he'd finally put his arms around her, pulling her closer to him. The way he smelled, like peppermint and cigarettes and French lavender laundry soap. The way he'd groaned a little when they stopped. She'd felt so rejected after their kiss yesterday, but maybe he'd changed his mind? She knew it was dangerous, but wasn't life about taking risks? She only hoped Eric felt the same way.

He was sprawled on a modern white lounge chair on the boat's deck, a bag of honey mustard pretzels at his side, when she arrived. He stood and brushed crumbs off his crisp chinos.

'Hey.'

'Hey,' she answered, standing at the water's edge. She'd quickly thrown on a black C&C California tee and hip-hugging Blue Cult jeans, hoping to look casual and unassuming, but now the outfit felt all wrong. Her shirt was too short and her pants were too low, so too much of her toned midriff winked up at him. It was too déclassé for Eric. She tried to cover it up with her hand. It didn't help that he looked absolutely gorgeous, his blondish-brown hair curling against the edges of his white polo shirt.

'Hey.' He smiled down at her.

'Hey again,' Brett said quietly.

They fell silent, looking at each other from a distance. Brett felt stupid – obviously he didn't feel the same way. Her stomach clunked inside of her, irritated that he would make her come here to tell her what she already knew: that they couldn't see each other anymore, blah, blah, blah. Fine, big fucking deal. She wanted it to be over quickly. And not *ever* see him again. She could resign from DC. Who cared if it looked good on your college applications? There were other ways to get into Brown.

'So this is what I've been thinking.' He interrupted her thoughts. 'You have one more year here. And you're seventeen. I'm twenty-three. That's like, six years.'

'Uh-huh,' Brett responded, twisting a piece of rope lying on one of the dock's pylons.

'Six years. Like, when we're in our twenties . . . you'll be, say, twenty-two, and I'll be twenty-eight. And when I'm fifty, you'll be forty-four.'

Brett snorted. 'So what are you saying?"

'I—' Eric started.

'No offense,' Brett retorted quickly, straightening up. 'But I'm not, like, holding out for you until I'm forty-four. Hopefully I'll be with a younger guy by then.'

Eric stared at her intensely. 'I don't think I could wait until you were forty-four.'

'Oh,' she replied, winding the rope around her finger so tightly that it began cutting off the circulation.

He stared at her, then sighed. 'Come into my cabin?'

Brett paused. She wasn't positive, but she suspected that this was about to be the biggest, most important moment of her life so far. Standing there, in a crappy T-shirt and her crappiest jeans, on a random Sunday after field hockey practice, slightly hungover, seventeen years old, a tiny pimple on the corner of her right cheek that was covered up with MAC concealer, AP bio homework to do . . . Her life a boring mess, otherwise. But if she wanted it to happen, the next moments could change her life forever.

'Yeah, I guess I can do that.' She smiled quietly to herself and ran her hands along the guide rails on the dock to climb aboard.

34

SOMETIMES A WAVERLY OWL MUST TAKE RISKS.

As Callie rounded the corner to Dumbarton, she saw Easy blocking the front doorway. Her first instinct was to turn in the other direction and go back to the playing fields.

But Easy saw her. 'Wait.' He started down the concrete steps. 'Come back.'

Callie turned reluctantly around. She flashed back to blurry images of the party last night: a mess of tequila bottles, Heath's ugly Celtic tattoo, Easy peeking out from the door beads, Heath's juvenile follow-up e-mail. Ever since the beginning of the year, everyone had been making fun of how Heath ponied all the girls; and sure, she'd been drunk, angry with Brett, and even angrier at Easy, but why had she let Heath pony her, too?

'Hey,' she answered gruffly.

'So. You have fun last night?' he asked, his eyebrows raised.

'I'm sorry.' She flapped her hands against her maroon and blue plaid hockey kilt. 'About the . . . you know. The thing. It was stupid. A drinking game.'

'It definitely caught me off guard.' Easy shuffled his foot against a pebble on the walkway. Seeing Easy awkward like this made Callie melt.

'That was a weird party.' She looked down.

Easy didn't answer.

'They weren't like that last year,' Callie went on. 'They were just fun.'

She sat down on the steps and pressed her knees together, fighting back an overwhelming urge to squeeze her eyes shut. 'I just want things with us to be like last year, too. We had so much fun.'

'Yeah,' Easy said softly.

'What's happened with us?'

'I don't know.'

'Maybe we could get it back.' Callie raised her head hopefully. 'Maybe if we just, I don't know. Go somewhere off campus and talk. Somewhere where nobody else is. Anywhere you want. I'll even go riding with you,' she added impulsively. Easy used to always try to get her to ride with him and she never had.

'You would?'

'If they don't boot me out of here, yeah.' She shifted on the step. 'I still don't know what Jenny's going to do. I mean, I don't think she wants to tell on me, but she doesn't want to get in trouble.'

Easy stared at his sneakers. 'I don't think Jenny *should* get in trouble.'

'Yeah, you've mentioned that.' Callie heard the edge in her own voice.

'I think you should take the blame. Jenny has nothing to do with this.'

'If I take the blame, I'll be expelled. You want that?'

Easy shook his head. 'No. I . . . I don't know. If only there was a way for neither of you to get in trouble . . .'

'I don't get it.' Callie stared at him. 'Why do you care so much whether or not she gets in trouble? You guys didn't even know each other until I . . .' Suddenly, it was as if a lightbulb had gone off over her head. What Brandon had told her after the pre-Black Saturday party. The writing on Jenny's arm. Heath's gossipy e-mail – *two people looking lovingly into each other's eyes*. They were both so open to flirting with each other when Callie asked them to.

Easy liked Jenny. Not because Callie had told him to like her, either. Because he really did.

Callie shoved her thumb into her mouth and turned away so that he couldn't see the expression on her face.

Easy watched her as she turned, wondering what she was thinking. How could he save both Jenny and Callie? The only thing he could think of might put his own place at Waverly in jeopardy. Was he man enough to do that?

Callie turned around again. 'I guess whatever happens happens.'

'Who knows. They still might kick me out.'

She was quiet for a second. 'I wish I could just, like, turn back time.'

Easy laid his hand over Callie's. 'I know,' he responded, thinking. This . . . whatever it was . . . with Jenny – it felt too big for him to understand. And maybe too scary. Looking at Callie, sitting on the steps in her field hockey kilt and after-practice flip-flops, her hair pulled back in a messy ponytail and without a stitch of makeup, she looked like a kid. Not a worldly, full-of-emotion adult. She was sweet and safe and something he understood. He hated to think of leaving her – whether that meant leaving her for Jenny or leaving Waverly completely. 'Maybe I can make that happen,' he said, squeezing his fingers around hers.

**WAVERLY OWLS SHOULD TRY NOT TO LET
THEIR BOYFRIENDS CATCH THEM WITH
ANOTHER GUY.**

An hour later, Brett walked back down the gang-plank, hugging herself, her mind reeling from what she'd just done.

Eric Dalton had taken off her clothes and kissed her everywhere. Then he'd taken his own clothes off slowly, as if he were in a strip club. Brett had never seen a guy take his clothes off *in the daylight*. He'd kept his eyes on her the whole time. They'd massaged each other and fooled around and then, just when things were going to go . . . further, she'd suddenly told him she needed some fresh air. Being with Eric was more than she had expected. More than her fantasy about him had been. It felt overwhelming. And not necessarily entirely in a good way. She needed to think.

And then, who did she see standing at the end of the dock?

Fuck.

'There she is,' Jeremiah muttered to himself. 'I thought you weren't into sailing.'

There were huge circles under his eyes. He was wearing jeans and a white T-shirt that said CBGB OMFUG, that punk club in Manhattan's East Village, and he was carrying a giant L.L. Bean duffel bag with his initials embroidered into one side. Brett felt a stab of guilt — something about Jeremiah, tough and cool, toting around a bag that no doubt his mommy had gotten monogrammed for him, seemed really vulnerable and sweet.

'Oh. Hey.'

'Hey?' Jeremiah shook his head. 'That's all you can say, *Hey*?'

'Well,' Brett tried to walk past him, but he stopped her with his arm. His hand gripped her bicep tightly. For a split second she was a little afraid and looked back to the boat for help. Then she realized — this was Jeremiah. She wrenched herself from his grasp. 'Don't touch me like that! Didn't you get my message?'

'What, so you break up with somebody on a voice mail?' he yelled back. 'That's real classy. I thought you were better than that.'

Brett didn't want to have this out right in front of Eric's boat — Eric, who had undressed very slowly. Eric, who had touched her deftly and maturely, not in the fumbling, grabby way boys her age did. Eric, who hadn't gotten mad when Brett covered herself with the Ralph Lauren paisley sheets and said they should stop. She started walking down the path back to campus. 'Fine.' She turned back. 'I'm breaking up with you in person, then. You happy?'

'I don't suppose you could give me any fucking reasons, could you?'

'Sure,' Brett scoffed. 'Did you really think this was serious? There. That's one.'

Jeremiah stopped. His eyes were all puffy and red. It looked as if he hadn't gone to bed yet.

'Yeah. I *did* think we were serious. Why else would I ask you to come to California with me?'

'Well . . .' She stared at the ground.

'But obviously there's somebody else,' he ventured. 'I was told to look for you here. This is some guy's boat, right? You were with some guy down there, on his boat, in his cabin? C'mon, Brett. That's a little trashy, don't you think?'

Brett prickled and narrowed her eyes. As if he were one to talk about low class, using that stupid townie accent! Then it hit her. 'Wait, who told you I'd be here?'

Jeremiah shrugged. 'Why does it matter?' He reached into his backpack and pulled out a pack of Camel Lights. 'The point is, somebody told me, and you made it really clear. So fuck it. It's your loss.'

He turned and loped back up to the green, an unlit cigarette dangling from his mouth.

'Wait,' Brett called hoarsely. A streak of nerves ran through her. 'Who told you I'd be—?'

But he was too far away to hear, and she didn't want to yell. She turned back and stared down at the docks. Eric's boat bobbed placidly on the water, as if it hadn't just almost been witness to the most life-changing moment of Brett's existence. With a few short steps, she could go back down there and climb back into bed next to Eric. They could drink wine and talk about things and he could make her feel better about everything. Then she could have sex with him, for her first time ever.

But she couldn't. And she wasn't sure why.

36

AN HONEST OWL IS A WAVERLY OWL.

On Monday morning, Jenny sat at the large, round oak table in Dean Marymount's office, a few minutes into her Disciplinary Committee meeting. The room smelled like a combination of old books and new paint. Easy sat only a few chairs away; Brett, Ryan, Celine, and the other DC members, as well as Mr Pardee, Mr Dalton, and Dean Marymount, sat in a line on the other side of the table, their hands folded and their eyes fixed carefully on her. Because it was DC members only, Callie wasn't allowed to be at the hearing. Jenny pictured Callie nervously smoking a whole pack of cigarettes inside Dumbarton right now, in anticipation of the verdict.

On the wall across from Jenny were silver-framed paint-ings created by Waverly's graduating classes, 1985 through present. They were handprints, in different poster-paint colors, each footnoted with the student's name. Even Waverly students' hands had a wealthy look about them. She wondered what hers would look like up there with the others. Then she wondered if she'd be at Waverly long enough to even to put her handprint on her class's painting.

Talk about down to the wire. She still hadn't decided what she was going to say in DC yet, and now it was time. Marymount, looking especially suburban in a navy argyle sweater vest under his maroon Waverly blazer and his gold wire-rimmed round glasses, licked his finger to turn the page of his steno pad. 'Okay. Mr Pardee, the notes here say that Mr Walsh was caught in Miss Humphrey's room. They were talking, and Mr Walsh was nearly naked. That's correct?'

'That's right,' confirmed Mr Pardee. 'I caught them, and it looked as if some sexual activity had taken place.' He looked down at the table then, color rising on his neck. Jenny bit the inside of her cheek.

Marymount swung his gaze over to Jenny. 'Miss Humphrey?'

This was it. Time to either sell out Callie, or sell out herself and her new life. She took a deep breath, even though she had no idea what she was about to say.

'It was all my fault.'

Everyone in the room turned to Easy. He cleared his throat.

'Excuse me?' Marymount asked.

'It was all my fault,' he repeated. 'See, I was looking for Callie. I'd been asleep, in my boxers, and I went over like that. I wandered into their room, but Callie wasn't there. So I started talking to Jenny, but she in no way invited me in. That's when Pardee caught us. It might have looked like Jenny and I were together, but we weren't. She really had nothing to do with this.'

Jenny's mouth fell open.

'I sat on her bed,' he went on. 'She didn't ask me to. I just went ahead and did it.'

Marymount ran his hand through his thinning sandy hair. 'Do you realize the repercussions of that? The inappropriateness?'

'Yeah.' Easy hung his head.

Jenny bit her lip and sat on her hands. The student part of the committee stared at her blankly, their faces completely devoid of emotion. Most likely because everyone was still hungover from Saturday night. Although she was trying her hardest to be unemotional, inside, she felt like a malfunctioning pinball machine. She was off the hook, but now Easy was in major trouble. What if he got kicked out? Would everyone blame her? More important, did Jenny risk losing the first boy she might even . . . love?'

Marymount straightened up and rolled his knuckles on the desk. 'Miss Humphrey? This is what happened?'

Jenny nodded slightly. It was true, after all. Sort of.

'Well, even so, this isn't the best way to start off the year, especially with your cheer at the field hockey game. I want you to report to my office next week.' Marymount frowned. 'I think we'll have to figure out something to keep you out of trouble.'

Jenny nodded. 'Okay.'

Marymount turned back to Easy. 'Just so we're clear. Mr Walsh, you're taking all the blame for this?'

Easy took a deep breath. He'd dreamed of this moment, the very second they *actually* kicked him out of Waverly. Somewhere inside of him it had always felt sort of inevitable. He'd imagined what he'd say, what he'd be wearing. He'd crazily imagined that he'd have on this red Mighty Morphin Power Rangers outfit he had as a kid and would wave around one of his dad's unloaded vintage rifles, just to freak them out a little. He'd have his oversized *Terminator* Dolce & Gabbana sunglasses on his forehead. He'd tell all the Waverly staff precisely what he thought of them and then he'd climb on Credo and ride off into the sunset.

But things never happened as you imagined them. Now he broke out in a cold sweat in his white Brooks Brothers button-down and maroon pressed Waverly jacket. He thought of all the stuff he'd miss if they booted him out. The owls. The way the sun set orange and purple over the Hudson. His favorite stained-glass window in the chapel. Playing soccer with Alan when they didn't feel like studying. The cafeteria's cherry pie and the cheerful cafeteria worker Mabel, who was from a little town near Lexington. Callie. Jenny. He'd miss everything he saw in Jenny.

'Well?' Marymount prompted again.

'Yes.' He nodded. 'I am.'

'Well, then,' Marymount continued in a small, disappointed voice. 'Committee, do we find Mr Walsh guilty? All in favor?'

Brett, Mr Dalton, Mr Pardee, and Benny raised their hands. The freshman and sophomore DC committee members shrugged apologetically but raised their hands too. Finally, Alan reluctantly raised his hand, and so did the two senior girl members.

A dreadful pause hung over the air as Marymount surveyed each of the DC members' hands. Easy stared at the floor.

Finally Marymount sighed. 'All right. This is what we're going to do. Mr Walsh, this is your absolute last warning. We're going to put you on probation. Again. Two weeks. You can't go to the stables unless there's an emergency with your horse. No town privileges, and no visitation privileges. You'll go to chapel, to class, and to meals, but that's *it*.'

He kept talking, but nobody could hear him. Alan, Benny, and the two senior girls let out collective, grateful sighs. Brett squeaked back in her chair and crossed her arms over her chest, trying not to smile.

'Wait,' Jenny whispered to no one in particular. 'What's happening?'

'It means the old bastard's letting me stay,' Easy murmured. But in his voice, she could tell how glad he was. And from the meaningful look he gave her, Jenny thought maybe, just maybe, it had something to do with her.

37

LOTS OF WAVERLY OWLS CAN BE
FABULOUS . . .
BUT ONLY ONE CAN BE IT.

Brett rifled through her gray nylon Hervé field hockey bag and pulled out a sixteen-ounce bottle of Gosling rum. 'We have to celebrate,' she announced dramatically. The three girls sat exhausted on the floor of Dumbarton dorm room 303, Jenny and Brett from the stress of DC, Callie from the stress of *not* being at DC.

Jenny watched as Brett poured rum slowly into each of their chipped Crate & Barrel highball glasses. She kind of felt like she had at the Black Saturday party – warm, gooey, and included. This was what she'd dreamed life at Waverly would be like, and now it was real. Her dreams had come true.

At least, she felt that with Brett. Callie still seemed a little cold. Sure, as soon as Jenny had come back in the room and told Callie the news, she'd quickly run over and given Jenny a huge hug, saying how eternally grateful she was that she hadn't named her. But there was still some unfinished business between them.

'To the new year at Waverly,' Brett toasted.

They clinked glasses.

'And,' Callie interjected, 'to us putting this whole Tinsley thing behind us.'

'Right,' Brett agreed.

'I didn't even know that was upsetting you guys so much,' Jenny ventured.

'It's a long story.'

'There were rumors,' Callie explained. 'People were talking about why Tinsley was kicked out. Some said I did it, others said Brett did. Neither of us knew what to believe.'

'Speaking of rumors,' Brett began. Jenny noticed that Brett's eyes were tinged pink, and her fingernails, normally polished and buffed to perfection, were bitten down to nubs. 'Um, did either of you hear anything about me and Eric Dalton?'

'No,' Callie answered a little too quickly. Jenny gave her a puzzled look.

Brett rolled her eyes. 'I mean, I know you both know. Anyway, I've been having this . . . this thing with Mr Dalton.'

'Did you sleep with him?' Callie asked.

'No. But I almost did.'

They were silent for a moment.

'But, um, Jeremiah caught me coming off his boat yesterday,' Brett continued evenly, pushing her hair behind her ear. Jenny noticed a huge hickey on her neck. 'And I'm wondering how he knew I'd be there.'

Jenny mashed her lips together and noticed Callie was doing the same thing. She hadn't said a word to anyone, but Callie certainly had. Although . . . how had Callie found out? Did Brett think she had told on her?

'I had no idea,' Callie repeated, not looking at Brett directly.

'Okay,' Brett muttered.

'Are you okay?' Jenny asked. 'With Mr Dalton and everything?'

Brett shrugged. She wasn't sure what to say. She wished she could be more adult and tell them the truth, that while she'd been watching Eric undress, she'd actually missed the way boys her age with fumbled around nervously, getting tangled in their clothes, like they couldn't believe their luck, being with a girl like Brett. Eric's obvious experience had freaked her out. She wished she could go back to him and confidently say, *Hey, big boy, take me now*. But she couldn't. She wasn't ready. Of course, she wanted to tell Callie and Jenny all of that, but she'd told Callie that she'd lost her virginity years ago to that Swiss boy in Gstaad. What would she think if Brett admitted the truth now?

The girls silently sipped their drinks, waiting for Brett to respond. Jenny leaned back. She felt lucky. She wasn't

Easy's girlfriend, but she knew that if anything ended up happening between them, it wouldn't feel wrong at all. It would feel exactly right. Now if only Callie would get back together with Brandon . . .

'Hey.' Callie broke the silence. 'I have an idea.' She scrambled to her feet and ran out of the room. Quickly, she returned holding a thick, red, leather-bound book. It said WAVERLY OWLS, 2000. 'The lounge has these dating back to the fifties.'

'An old yearbook?' Brett asked. 'We're not in this one yet.'

'No, but Mr Dalton is.' Callie smiled wryly.

'Oh my God, open it,' Jenny exclaimed.

They opened the book to seniors, then *D*, for *Dalton*. There he was, in a graduation tux, with that same, I'm-up-to-something-but-you'll-never-find-out smile. He did look five years younger but still every bit as cute. They stared at it in silence.

'I thought maybe we'd find out he was a huge dork who was obsessed with PlayStation and had a whole bunch of zits,' Callie admitted solemnly. 'I thought that might help.' She shrugged, 'That definitely doesn't appear to be the case.'

'Please,' Jenny countered. 'All we have to do is find his freshman yearbook. I guarantee he looked like a total freak. I mean, everybody looks dorky when they're a freshman.'

'Even you?' Callie asked good-naturedly.

'Oh, no. I was never a dork. You should see my pictures

from seventh grade. I had this Old Navy fleece thing happening. It was totally hot.'

'Ew.' Callie laughed.

'Yeah. When you meet my dad, he'll definitely show you pictures.'

Brett hit her with a pillow. 'You're so weird.'

Jenny started giggling and hit Brett back. A feather shot out of the pillow and landed on Callie's sticky MAC-lip-gloss-coated lip, causing Jenny to laugh even harder. Maybe it was the rum, but she felt manic.

Suddenly, there was a knock on the door. The girls froze.

'The rum,' Callie whispered. 'Under the bed.'

They scrambled to hide the cups and, in their hurry, even hid the 2000 yearbook. Callie flung the door open to see Marymount, Angelica Pardee, and Mr Pardee, all crowded by the wooden threshold.

Oh God, Jenny thought. *They've changed their minds. We're all getting expelled anyway. Shit, shit, shit.*

'This room is definitely big enough for four,' Angelica mused, looking around.

'All we'd need is an extra bed,' Mr Pardee added. 'There's already a free desk.'

Callie, Jenny, and Brett looked at one another. *Four?*

'Um, can we help you?' Brett asked. She tried to keep her mouth as closed as possible while she talked, so the teachers wouldn't smell her rummy breath.

'Girls,' Marymount announced, 'I have some interesting news that I think you'll be happy about.'

'What?' Callie was perplexed. 'You're sticking another girl in here with us?'

'Not just another girl.' Mr Pardee smiled. 'Your old friend Tinsley.'

All three roommates fell silent. Callie and Brett stared at each other, eyes widening. Jenny's eyes darted back and forth, between them. *Tinsley?*

'Wait,' Callie squeaked. 'What are you saying?'

'You heard us,' Marymount boomed. 'The faculty has decided to reinstate Tinsley.'

'And she's moving back in . . . here?'

'That's right.'

'Wow,' was all Brett could say. The other girls nodded.

'Jeepers,' Jenny added.

Jeepers pretty much said it all.

OwlNet   Instant Message Inbox

CallieVernon: You're just across the room, but I don't want Jenny to hear what I have to say.

BrettMesserschmidt: Okay, shoot.

CallieVernon: I don't know if there's room on this campus for Tinsley and Jenny.

BrettMesserschmidt: What do you mean?

CallieVernon: I know you know what I mean.

BrettMesserschmidt: Okay, yeah, they both have that . . . something. But maybe they'll be BFF?

CallieVernon: Or scratch each other's eyes out.

BrettMesserschmidt: It's going to be an interesting year . . .

CallieVernon: I'll say.

BrettMesserschmidt: How do u think Tinsley got back in, anyway?

CallieVernon: Maybe she gave Marymount a lap dance . . . I hear he likes that.

BrettMesserschmidt: You're so dirty.

CallieVernon: But that's why you love me!

BrettMesserschmidt: I do. For now, anyway . . .